Romance Beyond the Shadows

Candy Christie

Author

Candy Christie is a passionate storyteller and emerging author in the romance genre. With a deep love for weaving intricate tales of love, betrayal, and redemption, Candy has quickly captured the hearts of readers with her evocative and heartfelt narratives.

Candy's journey into writing began at an early age, inspired by the timeless classics and the romantic novels she devoured. Her unique ability to create relatable, multidimensional characters and place them in richly detailed settings has garnered her a dedicated readership.

"Romance Beyond the Shadows" is the latest addition to her growing collection of novels, following the success of her earlier works. In this series, she explores the complexities of human relationships, the impact of the past on the present, and the enduring power of love to transform lives.

When she's not writing, Candy enjoys traveling, exploring historical sites, and immersing herself in new cultures. These experiences often find their way into her stories, adding depth and authenticity to her writing. She lives in a cozy cottage with her beloved pets and an ever-growing collection of books.

Candy Christie invites you to join her on this journey of love, mystery, and self-discovery. Connect with her on social media for updates on her latest projects and a glimpse into her creative process.

Candy Christie

Disclaimer

This is a work of fiction. Names, characters, places, and incidents are either the product of the author's imagination or used fictitiously. Any resemblance to actual persons, living or dead, events, or locales is entirely coincidental.

The author has taken artistic liberties to create a compelling narrative, and the historical and supernatural elements depicted are purely fictional. The mansion, its history, and the events described within these pages are products of the author's creative process.

This book is intended for mature audiences only. Reader discretion is advised. The content includes themes and scenes that may not be suitable for younger readers.

All rights reserved. No part of this book may be reproduced, distributed, or transmitted in any form or by any means, without the prior written permission of the author, except in the case of brief quotations embodied in critical reviews and certain other noncommercial uses permitted by copyright law.

For any permissions requests, please contact the author through the publisher.

Candy Christie

Preface

In the grand halls of an old mansion, beneath the whispers of its long-forgotten past, lies a story of love, redemption, and the unwavering strength of the human spirit. "Romance Beyond the Shadows" is a tale that transcends time, bridging the gap between the present and the echoes of history. It is a testament to the power of love to heal wounds, forge unbreakable bonds, and illuminate even the darkest corners of our hearts.

As the author of this novel, I, Candy Christie, am deeply honored to share with you the journey of Emily, Daniel, Grace, and Jack. Their lives intertwine in ways that are both surprising and deeply moving, revealing the resilience and courage that love can inspire. Through their trials and triumphs, they learn that true love is not without its challenges, but it is these very challenges that make them love all the more profound.

This story is more than just a romantic saga; it is an exploration of trust, betrayal, and the capacity for forgiveness. It delves into the mysteries of the past, uncovering secrets that shape the present and influence the future. The characters you will meet in these pages are flawed and human, yet it is their imperfections that make their journey so compelling.

I invite you to step into the world of this mansion, to walk its shadowed corridors and sunlit gardens, to feel the weight of its history and the hope of its future. As you turn each page, may you be reminded of the enduring power of love and the endless possibilities that await those who dare to open their hearts.

Thank you for joining me on this journey. May Emily, Daniel, Grace, and Jack inspire you as much as they have inspired me.

With heartfelt gratitude,

Candy Christie

Chapter 1: The Calm Before the Storm

The morning sun streamed through the tall windows of the mansion, casting a golden glow on the polished wooden floors. The grand hall, once a place of shadows and secrets, now bustled with life and energy. Emily stood at the entrance, her heart swelling with pride as she took in the scene before her.

Artists from across the country had gathered, their works adorning the walls and easels scattered throughout the hall. The air buzzed with excitement and chatter; the hum of creativity palpable. Emily glanced around, her eyes landing on Daniel, who was engaged in conversation with a group of artists. His face lit up with enthusiasm as he discussed the details of their work, his passion for art and community shining through.

Emily made her way through the crowd, stopping to admire a striking painting of a stormy seascape. The artist, a young woman with bright eyes and a shy smile, noticed her interest and stepped forward.

"Do you like it?" she asked, her voice tinged with both hope and nervousness.

"It's beautiful," Emily replied warmly. "The way you've captured the movement and power of the waves is truly impressive."

The young woman beamed, her cheeks flushing with pride. "Thank you so much. It means a lot to hear that from you."

Emily smiled, giving the artist a reassuring nod before moving on. She could hardly believe how far they had come. The mansion, once a place of sorrow and fear, had been transformed into a thriving hub of creativity and community. It was a testament to the power of love and determination.

As she continued to weave through the crowd, Emily caught sight of an older man standing in front of a portrait of a young couple. The painting was vibrant and full of life, the couple's love for each other evident in their expressions.

"That one's my favorite," the man said, noticing Emily's gaze. "It reminds me of my late wife. We used to come here when we were young, before the mansion fell into disrepair."

Emily's heart ached with a bittersweet tenderness. "I'm so glad you could come back and see it now. We've worked hard to restore it to its former glory."

The man nodded; his eyes misty with memories. "You've done a wonderful job. Thank you for bringing it back to life."

Emily felt a lump form in her throat as she thanked the man and continued her journey through the hall. She found Daniel near the stage, where a local band was setting up to perform. He turned and saw her approaching, his face lighting up with a smile.

"Emily, this is incredible," he said, pulling her into a warm embrace. "Look at all these people, all this talent. We've really done something special here."

Emily rested her head against his chest, feeling the steady beat of his heart. "I couldn't have done it without you, Daniel. This is our dream come true."

Daniel tilted her chin up, looking deeply into her eyes. "I love you, Emily. More than anything. And I'm so proud of what we've accomplished together."

Tears of joy welled up in Emily's eyes as she leaned in for a tender kiss. Their love had not only transformed their lives but had also brought new life to the mansion and the community.

As the band began to play, filling the hall with music, Emily and Daniel moved to the center of the room. They danced together, lost in each other's arms, surrounded by the beauty and creativity they had helped foster. The world around them faded away, leaving only the two of them, united by love and the promise of a bright future.

In that moment, everything felt perfect. The mansion was alive with art and laughter, a beacon of hope and inspiration. Emily and Daniel's journey had brought them to this point, and they knew that whatever challenges lay ahead, they would face them together, stronger than ever.

As the evening wore on, the hall continued to buzz with activity. Guests mingled, sharing stories and admiring the artwork, while the band played on. Emily and Daniel moved through the crowd, greeting friends and newcomers alike, their hearts full of joy and gratitude.

After the grand ball room party Emily and Daniel were tired and were lying on the bed. Maid were doing the cleaning of the ball room. Daniel looked at Emily and kissed her, thanking her for a great night. Emily smiled, her cheeks blushing. Daniel told her she looked the most beautiful among all. Emily blushed even more and leaned in to kiss Daniel back. Their lips met, and it was a passionate kiss. Daniel's hands found Emily's waist, pulling her closer to him. Emily wrapped her arms around Daniel's neck, deepening the kiss.

Emily sat up, straddling Daniel's waist. She looked down at him, her eyes sparkling with desire. Daniel's hands traveled up Emily's thighs, feeling the softness of her skin. Emily leaned down, her hair creating a curtain around them. She kissed Daniel deeply, her tongue exploring his mouth. Daniel's hands moved to Emily's ass, squeezing it gently. Emily moaned into the kiss, grinding her hips against Daniel's.

Daniel's hands moved to the buttons of Emily's dress, undoing them one by one. Emily's dress fell open, revealing her lacy bra and panties. Daniel's eyes widened, taking in the sight of Emily's body. Emily leaned back, allowing Daniel to remove her dress. Daniel's hands moved to Emily's bra, unclasping it and letting it fall to the side. Emily's breasts were perfect, her nipples hard with desire. Daniel leaned up, taking one of Emily's nipples into his mouth. Emily moaned, running her fingers through Daniel's hair.

Emily stood up, removing her panties. Daniel's eyes traveled down Emily's body, taking in the sight of her shaved pussy. Daniel's dick was hard, straining against his pants. Emily removed Daniel's pants, freeing his dick. Daniel's dick was huge, at least 8 inches long. Emily's pussy was already wet, ready for Daniel's dick. Emily sat down on Daniel's lap, her legs crisscrossed around his waist. Daniel's dick was at her entrance, and Emily slowly lowered herself onto it. Daniel's dick filled her up, and Emily moaned with pleasure. Daniel's hands moved to Emily's hips, guiding her up and down on his dick.

Emily leaned down, her arms around Daniel's shoulders. Daniel's dick was deep inside her, and Emily could feel every inch of it. Daniel's hands moved to Emily's ass, squeezing it gently. Emily moaned, grinding her hips against Daniel's. Daniel's thrusts became deeper, and Emily could feel herself getting closer to orgasm. Daniel's fingers moved to Emily's ass, gently massaging it. Emily moaned louder, her orgasm building. Daniel's fingers moved to Emily's pussy, feeling her wetness. Emily's orgasm hit her like a wave, and she moaned loudly, her pussy clenching around Daniel's dick. Daniel's orgasm followed, and he filled Emily's pussy with his cum. Emily collapsed onto Daniel, her head on his chest. Daniel's arms wrapped around Emily, holding her close.

The calm before the storm was a moment of pure, unfiltered happiness, a testament to the power of love and the beauty of new beginnings. And as the night ended, Emily and Daniel knew that this was just the beginning of their incredible journey together.

Chapter 2: Unwelcome Arrival

The art exhibition at the mansion had been in full swing for hours, a beautiful cacophony of voices, laughter, and the soft murmur of admiration for the displayed works. Emily moved through the crowd, her heart light and her spirits high. The mansion, once a symbol of darkness and despair, now thrived as a vibrant community hub, filled with creativity and hope.

She was admiring a particularly striking sculpture when a hush fell over the crowd. Emily turned, her eyes scanning the room to see what had caused the sudden change in atmosphere. Her heart skipped a beat, and her breath caught in her throat as she saw him.

Michael stood at the entrance of the grand hall, his presence commanding and confident. His eyes scanned the room, and when they landed on Emily, a smirk tugged at the corner of his lips. Michael, her former lover, the man who had shattered her trust and stolen her work, was here.

Emily felt a rush of emotions—anger, betrayal, and a pang of fear—but she quickly composed herself. She was no longer the broken woman who had fled the city to escape him. She was stronger now, determined, and she had Daniel by her side.

Michael had no idea that Emily would be at this art exhibition. She wasn't exactly his girlfriend, but they'd fucked enough times to consider each other X lovers. Michael's eyes widened as he noticed her in the crowd, her fuller body and glowing skin a welcome sight. He'd always had a thing for her curves, and the way she moved with such confidence was a turn-on.

Michael couldn't take his eyes off Emily as she made her way through the exhibition, admiring the various pieces of art on display. He couldn't help but feel a growing lust for her, and he wanted to have her again. He made his way over to her, his heart racing with excitement.

"Emily," Michael said, his voice low and seductive. "I didn't know you'd be here."

Daniel appeared beside her, sensing her tension. "Who is that?" he asked, his voice low and concerned.

"Michael," Emily replied, her voice steady despite the turmoil inside her. "He's the one who betrayed me, the one who stole my work."

Daniel's eyes darkened with protectiveness. "What is he doing here?"

Emily took a deep breath, her resolve hardening. "I don't know, but I'm not going to let him ruin this for me. I'm going to confront him and show him that he no longer has any power over me."

With Daniel by her side, Emily made her way through the crowd towards Michael. The room seemed to part for her, the guests sensing the significance of the moment. When she reached him, she stood tall, meeting his gaze with unwavering confidence.

"Michael," she said, her voice strong and clear. "What are you doing here?"

Michael's smirk widened, his eyes gleaming with a mix of surprise and amusement. "Emily, it's been a while. I heard about the exhibition and thought I'd see what all the fuss was about. Seems like you've done well for yourself."

Emily clenched her fists, but she kept her composure. "I have. And I'm not going to let you ruin it. Whatever you're here for, it won't work."

Michael chuckled, a condescending sound that grated on her nerves. "I'm not here to cause trouble, Emily. I'm here to compete. I've entered the competition."

A murmur of shock rippled through the crowd. Emily felt her heart pound in her chest, but she refused to back down. "Fine. Then we'll see who truly deserves to win."

Daniel stepped forward, his presence a solid pillar of support. "Emily's right. This is her moment, and nothing you do can take that away from her."

Michael glanced at Daniel, his expression turning cold. "And who might you be?"

"Daniel Hayes," he replied firmly. "Emily's partner and the co-host of this exhibition."

Michael's eyes narrowed, but he didn't respond. Instead, he turned back to Emily, his smirk returning. "May the best artist win, then."

Emily nodded, her resolve stronger than ever. "May the best artist win."

The competition took place in a beautiful public square near the mansion, surrounded by the town's historic buildings and vibrant market stalls. Easels were set up in a semi-circle, each artist given a space to create their masterpiece. The air buzzed with excitement and anticipation as locals and visitors gathered to watch the artists at work.

Emily set up her easel, her mind focused on the task at hand. She chose to paint a scene that had always brought her peace—the view of the mansion's garden at sunset, a place where she and Daniel had shared many quiet, happy moments. As she worked, she felt the familiar flow of creativity, her brush moving with confidence and purpose.

Michael was positioned a few easels away, his gaze occasionally flicking over to Emily. She could feel his presence, a dark shadow at the edge of her consciousness, but she refused to let it distract her. This was her moment to shine, to reclaim her pride and prove her talent.

Daniel stayed close, offering quiet words of encouragement and support. His presence was a steadying force, grounding her and giving her the strength she needed.

As the hours passed, the square filled with spectators, their admiration and curiosity palpable. Emily poured her heart into her painting, the colors and shapes coming together to create a vivid, lifelike image of the garden. When she finally stepped back to assess her work, she felt a surge of satisfaction. This was her best work yet, a true reflection of her skill and passion.

The judges moved from easel to easel, examining each piece with keen eyes and thoughtful expressions. When they reached Emily's painting, they paused, their faces lighting up with admiration. She held her breath, waiting for their verdict.

Finally, the head judge turned to her, a smile spreading across his face. "Emily Turner," he announced, his voice carrying through the crowd. "Your work is exceptional. You are the winner of this competition."

A wave of applause and cheers erupted from the crowd. Emily felt tears of joy and relief fill her eyes. She had done it. She had faced her past and emerged victorious.

Michael stood at the edge of the crowd, his expression a mix of shock and grudging admiration. Emily met his gaze, and for the first time, she felt a sense of closure. He no longer had any power over her.

Daniel rushed to her side, lifting her in a jubilant embrace. "You did it, Emily! I'm so proud of you."

Emily laughed through her tears, her heart soaring. "We did it, Daniel. Together."

As the celebration continued, Emily felt a profound sense of peace and triumph. She had reclaimed her pride, her talent, and her future. And with Daniel by her side, she knew that nothing could ever take that away from her again.

The calm before the storm had passed, and Emily emerged stronger, ready to face whatever challenges lay ahead with the love and support of the man who had helped her rediscover her strength.

Chapter 3: Jack's Discovery

The morning sunlight filtered through the lace curtains of the mansion, casting a warm glow across the polished wooden floors. Emily and Daniel were sitting at the grand dining table, enjoying a quiet breakfast together. The tranquility of the mansion, now a haven of creativity and community, was a stark contrast to its tumultuous past.

As they sipped their coffee and discussed the upcoming events, there was a gentle knock on the door. Emily looked up, curiosity piqued. "I wonder who that could be," she said, setting her cup down.

Daniel stood up, his eyes twinkling with anticipation. "Let's find out."

They walked to the entrance together, opening the door to reveal a tall, handsome man with dark hair and a warm smile. He carried a leather satchel slung over his shoulder, and his eyes sparkled with excitement.

"Good morning," the man said, his voice rich and inviting. "I'm Jack, a local historian. I've come to share some intriguing information about the mansion's history."

Before Emily or Daniel could respond, the beautiful maid appeared from behind them. Her name was Grace, a young woman with striking features and a quiet grace that belied her mysterious past. She smiled warmly at Jack, her eyes meeting his with a spark of recognition.

"Good morning, Mr. Jack," Grace said, her voice soft and welcoming. "Please, come in."

Jack's smile widened as he stepped inside, his gaze lingering on Grace for a moment before turning to Emily and Daniel. "Thank you. I've been researching the mansion for years, and I believe I've uncovered some fascinating details that could shed light on its hidden secrets."

Emily and Daniel exchanged a glance, their curiosity piqued. "We'd love to hear what you've discovered," Emily said, leading Jack to the library.

The library was a grand room filled with shelves of old books and artifacts. The large windows let in plenty of natural light, illuminating the rich mahogany furniture and the intricate details of the room. Grace followed them in, quietly taking a seat by the window.

Jack placed his satchel on the table and began to pull out a series of old documents, maps, and photographs. "The mansion has a long and storied history," he began, spreading the documents out before them. "While Isabella and Jonathan's story has been resolved, there are still other mysteries tied to this place."

He pointed to a faded photograph of an unfamiliar couple standing in front of the mansion. "This is a photograph of Samuel and Eliza, previous owners of the mansion in the early 20th century. They were known to have dabbled in the occult and performed rituals in the hidden rooms of this very house."

Emily leaned closer, her heart racing with excitement. "We've heard bits and pieces about the mansion's history after Isabella and Jonathan, but we never knew the full extent."

Jack nodded, his eyes darkening with the weight of the past. "Samuel and Eliza were obsessed with immortality and power. They believed they could summon entities from beyond to grant them eternal life. The rituals they performed were dangerous, and they unleashed something malevolent that still lingers here."

Daniel's brow furrowed as he studied the documents. "So, the mansion's history is even darker than we thought?"

"Yes," Jack replied. "And I believe there are hidden rooms and passages within the mansion that hold the key to uncovering what they did and how to stop it."

Grace, who had been quietly listening, spoke up. "I've heard whispers about these hidden rooms. My grandmother used to work here and told me stories about secret passages and strange happenings."

Emily and Daniel exchanged a glance, their determination renewed. "We need to uncover the truth," Emily said. "For the sake of the mansion and everyone who lives here."

Jack smiled, his admiration for Emily and Daniel evident. "I'd be honored to help you. Together, we can piece together the full story and hopefully rid the mansion of any lingering darkness."

As they delved deeper into the documents, Grace excused herself to attend to her duties. Jack watched her leave, a thoughtful expression on his face. "Grace is remarkable," he said softly. "She seems to know so much about the mansion."

Emily smiled, sensing the connection between Jack and Grace. "She's been a great help to us. Her knowledge and intuition are invaluable."

Jack nodded, his eyes lingering on the door through which Grace had disappeared. "I'd like to speak with her more, if that's alright. I believe she might hold some of the keys to unlocking the mansion's secrets."

Daniel clapped Jack on the shoulder, a friendly gesture of encouragement. "We're glad to have you on board, Jack. Let's uncover these secrets together."

The hours flew by as they poured over the documents, each discovery bringing them closer to understanding the mansion's dark past. Emily and Daniel felt a renewed sense of purpose, their bond growing stronger with each revelation.

Later that evening, as the sun set and cast a warm glow over the mansion, Emily and Daniel took a moment to reflect on their progress. They stood on the veranda, watching the vibrant colors of the sunset fade into twilight.

"This is just the beginning," Daniel said, his voice filled with determination. "We're going to uncover the truth and bring peace to this place."

Emily nodded, leaning into his embrace. "And we'll do it together, with Jack and Grace's help."

As the stars began to twinkle in the night sky, Emily felt a sense of hope and excitement for the journey ahead. The mansion's dark past was slowly coming to light, and with it, the promise of a brighter future.

Jack's discovery had set them on a new path, one filled with mystery, intrigue, and the unbreakable bond of love. And as they stood together, ready to face whatever challenges lay ahead, Emily knew that they were stronger than ever, united by their shared determination to uncover the truth and create a legacy of love and light.

Chapter 4: Shadows Awaken

The mansion, once a place of darkness and despair, had been transformed into a thriving hub of creativity and community. Yet, beneath its newfound warmth, a chilling unease began to stir. Emily couldn't shake the feeling that something sinister was lurking in the shadows.

It started with small, inexplicable events. Objects moved on their own, doors creaked open without a breeze, and strange whispers echoed through the halls at night. At first, Emily dismissed these occurrences as mere coincidences, but as they grew more frequent and unsettling, she couldn't ignore them any longer.

One night, as she lay in bed beside Daniel, she was jolted awake by a cold, eerie sensation. Her heart pounded as she glanced at the clock—it was just past midnight. She turned to Daniel, who was sound asleep, his breathing deep and steady. Emily took a deep breath, trying to calm herself, but then she felt it—a weight on the bed, as if someone was sitting right next to her.

Panic surged through her veins. She reached out to shake Daniel awake, but her hand froze in mid-air when she heard a faint, almost inaudible whisper close to her ear.

"Emily..."

Her breath caught in her throat, and she clutched the blanket tightly. The room was dark, the only light coming from the moon filtering through the curtains. Summoning all her courage, she turned her head slowly, her eyes scanning the room for any sign of an intruder. But there was nothing—only shadows dancing in the corners.

Daniel stirred beside her, his arm wrapping protectively around her waist. "Emily, are you okay?" he murmured, still half-asleep.

She took a shaky breath, leaning into his comforting presence. "I... I think someone was on the bed," she whispered, her voice trembling.

Daniel immediately sat up, his eyes wide with concern. "What do you mean? Are you sure?"

"I felt something," Emily insisted, her voice barely audible. "And I heard a whisper. It said my name."

Daniel switched on the bedside lamp, casting a warm glow over the room. He scanned the space, his jaw clenched. "There's no one here now," he said, his voice firm but gentle. "But we can't ignore this. Something's happening."

The next morning, they gathered the community for a meeting in the grand hall. The room was filled with concerned faces, the atmosphere heavy with unease. Daniel addressed the group, his voice steady and reassuring.

"We've been experiencing some strange occurrences in the mansion," he began. "Objects moving on their own, whispers at night, and... well, Emily had a particularly unsettling experience last night."

Murmurs spread through the crowd, a mix of fear and curiosity. Jack, the local historian, stepped forward, his expression serious. "It seems the mansion's past is still affecting the present. We need to investigate further and understand what's causing these disturbances."

Grace, the maid, who had been quietly listening, spoke up. "My grandmother used to tell me stories about spirits and entities that were bound to places like this. Maybe we need to find a way to communicate with them and understand what they want."

Emily felt a chill run down her spine at Grace's words. The idea of communicating with spirits was both terrifying and intriguing. She looked at Daniel, who nodded in agreement. "We need to get to the bottom of this," he said firmly. "For the sake of everyone here."

Over the next few days, the strange occurrences continued. Doors would slam shut without warning, cold drafts would sweep through the halls, and eerie whispers filled the night air. The community grew increasingly uneasy, their once-thriving hub now overshadowed by fear.

One evening, Emily decided to take a long, hot shower to try and relax. She turned on the water, watching the steam rise and fill the bathroom. As she stepped under the warm spray, she closed her eyes, letting the water wash away her worries. But her sense of peace was short-lived.

Suddenly, the water turned icy cold, causing her to gasp in shock. She reached for the handle to adjust the temperature, but before she could touch it, the water turned a deep, blood-red color. Emily's heart raced as she stared in horror at the crimson liquid pouring over her.

She stumbled out of the shower, grabbing a towel and wrapping it around herself. Her breath came in short, panicked bursts as she watched the water continue to flow red. "Daniel!" she screamed, her voice echoing through the bathroom.

Daniel burst into the room moments later, his face a mask of concern and holding the naked body of Emily close to her. Emilys towel fell to ground as she hugged him. "What's wrong, Emily?"

She pointed to the shower, her hands shaking. "The water... it turned cold and red. Like blood."

Daniel's eyes widened in shock as he approached the shower. He reached out cautiously, touching the water. It was clear again, as if nothing had happened. He turned to Emily; his expression grim. "We need to get to the bottom of this. There's something very wrong here."

Another evening, as Emily was working in her art studio, she felt a cold presence behind her. She turned around slowly, her heart pounding, but saw nothing. Determined not to let fear consume her, she picked up her brush and continued painting. But as she worked, the whispers grew louder, more insistent.

"Emily... help us..."

She dropped her brush, her hands shaking. The voice was clearer now, and it filled her with a sense of urgency. She knew she couldn't ignore it any longer.

That night, Emily, Daniel, Jack, and Grace gathered in the library. They had decided to perform a séance, hoping to communicate with the spirits and understand what they wanted. The room was dimly lit by candles, their flickering light casting eerie shadows on the walls.

Grace took the lead, her calm demeanor a source of strength for the group. "We need to open ourselves to the spirits," she explained. "Let them know we're here to help."

They joined hands, forming a circle around the table. Grace began to chant softly, calling upon the spirits to reveal themselves. The air grew colder, and a palpable tension filled the room.

Suddenly, the table shook, and the candles flickered wildly. Emily felt a rush of cold air sweep past her, and then she heard it—the whisper, clear and desperate.

"Emily... free us..."

Her heart raced as she squeezed Daniel's hand. "We're here to help," she said aloud, her voice trembling. "Tell us what you need."

The room fell silent, the air heavy with anticipation. Then, the whisper returned, stronger this time.

"The ritual... unfinished... find the key..."

Jack's eyes widened as he looked at the others. "The hidden rooms," he said urgently. "We need to find them and complete the ritual."

Determined to bring peace to the mansion and its restless spirits, they began their search. They scoured the mansion, uncovering hidden passages and secret chambers that had been forgotten for decades. Each discovery brought them closer to understanding the truth.

As they delved deeper into the mansion's secrets, Emily and Daniel's bond grew stronger. They faced their fears together, their love a beacon of light in the darkness. And with Jack and Grace's unwavering support, they knew they could overcome whatever challenges lay ahead.

The shadows had awakened, but Emily was determined to bring light to the darkness. With courage and love as their guide, they would uncover the truth and finally bring peace to the mansion and its haunted past.

Chapter 5: The Maid's Secret

The mansion was shrouded in an eerie stillness, a stark contrast to the bustling activity of the previous days. The unsettling events had left everyone on edge, and Emily and Daniel were determined to uncover the source of the disturbances. They had gathered in the library, poring over old documents and maps, hoping to find a clue that would explain the recent occurrences.

Grace, the maid, had been a quiet but invaluable presence. Her calm demeanor and intuitive understanding of the mansion's secrets had been a comfort to Emily. This evening, as the sun dipped below the horizon and the shadows grew longer, Grace approached Emily with a somber expression.

"Miss Emily," she began, her voice trembling slightly, "there is something I need to tell you."

Emily looked up from the dusty tome she had been reading, her curiosity piqued. "What is it, Grace?"

Grace glanced around nervously, her eyes darting to the door as if she expected someone to overhear. "It's about the mansion... and my family."

Daniel, who had been examining an old map, joined them, his expression concerned. "What do you mean, Grace?"

Taking a deep breath, Grace began to unravel the tale that had been passed down through her family for generations. "My grandmother used to work here, long before the mansion fell into disrepair. She told me stories about the Montgomery's and the dark secrets they kept. But there was more... much more."

Emily and Daniel listened intently as Grace recounted the history of the mansion. "My great great grandmother was close to Isabella Montgomery. They were like sisters. When Isabella and Jonathan performed those rituals, my grandmother was there. She witnessed everything."

Grace's voice grew softer, filled with emotion. "But it wasn't just the Montgomery's who were involved. My family... we were part of it too. My great-great-grandmother was a healer, and she knew ancient rites that were meant to protect and cleanse. Isabella asked for her help when the rituals went wrong."

Daniel frowned; his brow furrowed. "What happened?"

Grace took another deep breath, her eyes filled with sorrow. "The rituals were supposed to bind Isabella and Jonathan's love for eternity, but instead, they unleashed a dark force that cursed the mansion. My great-great-grandmother tried to reverse it, but she couldn't. The spirit that was summoned was too powerful, too malevolent."

Emily felt a chill run down her spine. "So, the disturbances we're experiencing now... they're because of this spirit?"

Grace nodded. "Yes. And there's more. My grandmother kept a journal, detailing everything that happened. It's hidden in a secret room behind the library. She believed that if anyone could find a way to banish the spirit, it would be through the knowledge in that journal."

Determined to find the journal, Emily and Daniel followed Grace to the back of the library. Grace pushed aside a heavy bookcase, revealing a narrow passageway. They entered the hidden room, their footsteps echoing in the silence.

The room was small and dimly lit, filled with old books and artifacts. In the center of the room was a wooden chest, intricately carved with symbols that seemed to glow in the faint light. Grace knelt beside the chest and carefully opened it, revealing the journal inside.

Emily picked up the journal, her hands trembling slightly. The leather cover was worn, the pages yellowed with age. She opened it, and the scent of old paper filled the air. The first page was filled with elegant handwriting, detailing the events that had led to the mansion's curse.

As they read through the journal, Emily and Daniel realized the extent of the dark forces at play. The spirit that had been summoned was not just malevolent; it was vengeful. It fed on fear and despair, growing stronger with each passing year.

"We have to find a way to banish this spirit," Daniel said, his voice firm. "We can't let it continue to haunt this place."

Grace nodded; her eyes filled with determination. "My great-grandmother's notes are in the back of the journal. She believed that there was a way to reverse the curse, but it would require great sacrifice."

Emily's heart ached as she thought about the sacrifices that had already been made. But she knew that they couldn't give up. They had to fight for the future of the mansion and the community that had grown around it.

With the journal in hand, Emily, Daniel, and Grace returned to the main library. They spread out the old maps and documents, cross-referencing the information in the journal with the mansion's layout. As they worked, a plan began to take shape.

"We'll need to perform a cleansing ritual," Emily said, her voice steady. "One that will banish the spirit for good. But we'll need help."

Daniel nodded. "We'll gather the community. Everyone will need to be involved."

Grace smiled, her eyes shining with hope. "My family has always believed in the power of unity and love. Together, we can overcome this darkness."

As the night wore on, they continued to work, their determination unwavering. Emily felt a sense of peace settle over her, knowing that they were on the right path. They were not just fighting for themselves, but for everyone who had ever called the mansion home.

The shadows had awakened, but Emily, Daniel, and Grace were ready to face them head-on. With love, courage, and the strength of their community, they would banish the darkness and restore the mansion to its former glory.

The dawn of a new day was approaching, and with it, the promise of a brighter future. Together, they would overcome the challenges ahead and create a legacy of love and light that would shine for generations to come.

Chapter 6: The Spirit's Wrath

The mansion, once a haven of creativity and community, had become a battleground. The malevolent spirit's presence had grown stronger, its wrath manifesting in increasingly violent and chaotic ways. Doors slammed shut with bone-jarring force, windows shattered without warning, and eerie whispers filled the halls, sowing fear and unease among the residents.

Emily and Daniel, determined to uncover the spirit's origins and put an end to its reign of terror, enlisted the help of Jack and Grace. Together, they delved deeper into the mansion's dark history, searching for clues that could explain the spirit's fury and reveal a way to banish it for good.

One evening, as the four of them gathered in the library, the air thick with tension, Emily's phone rang. She glanced at the screen and saw that it was her aunt, Margaret, who lived six hours away. Emily's heart skipped a beat. Margaret rarely called, and when she did, it was usually important.

"Excuse me," Emily said, stepping away from the group to take the call. "Aunt Margaret? Is everything alright?"

Margaret's voice was weak and frail, filled with a fatigue that sent a shiver down Emily's spine. "Emily, dear... I'm very ill. I need you to come visit me. Please, it's urgent."

Emily's heart sank. Margaret had always been like a second mother to her, and the thought of her being seriously ill was almost too much to bear. "Of course, Aunt Margaret. I'll leave right away."

After ending the call, Emily returned to the library, her face pale and her eyes filled with concern. Daniel immediately noticed her distress. "What's wrong, Emily?"

"It's my Aunt Margaret," she replied, her voice trembling. "She's very ill and needs me to visit her. I have to go."

Daniel's expression softened with understanding. "Of course. We'll manage here. Your family needs you."

Jack and Grace nodded in agreement. "We'll continue our research," Jack said. "Go be with your aunt. We'll keep you updated on our progress."

Emily felt a rush of gratitude for their support. "Thank you. I'll be back as soon as I can."

With a heavy heart, Emily packed a bag and set off for Margaret's house. The drive was long and exhausting, but her thoughts were consumed by worry for her aunt and the growing danger at the mansion. The further she drove, the more the tension seemed to lift, though a part of her remained tethered to the events unfolding back home.

When she finally arrived at Margaret's quaint cottage, the sun had long since set. Emily hurried inside, finding her aunt resting in bed, looking frail but managing a weak smile.

"Emily, dear… thank you for coming," Margaret said, her voice barely above a whisper.

Emily sat by her bedside, taking her hand gently. "Of course, Aunt Margaret. I'm here now. What's going on? How can I help?"

Margaret sighed, her eyes closing briefly. "I've been feeling unwell for some time now. The doctors aren't sure what it is. I just wanted to see you… to talk to you…"

Tears welled up in Emily's eyes. "I'm here, Aunt Margaret. We can talk about anything."

As the hours passed, Emily listened to her aunt's stories and memories, cherishing every moment they had together. Despite her worry for the mansion and the spirit's growing power, being with Margaret provided a sense of solace and grounding.

Back at the mansion, Daniel, Jack, and Grace continued their investigation. The spirit's attacks grew more frequent and aggressive, filling the mansion with a palpable sense of dread. One night, as they pored over old documents and artifacts, a sudden gust of wind blew through the library, extinguishing the candles and plunging the room into darkness.

"Did you feel that?" Jack whispered, his voice tinged with fear.

Grace nodded, her eyes wide. "The spirit is here. It's trying to stop us."

Determined not to be deterred, Daniel relit the candles, their flickering light casting eerie shadows on the walls. "We have to keep going. We're close to finding out the truth."

As they continued their work, they discovered a hidden compartment in one of the ancient bookshelves. Inside, they found a set of old letters, yellowed with age and written in a flowing, elegant script. The letters detailed the story of a woman named Eliza, who had lived in the mansion over a century ago. She had been deeply in love with a man named Samuel, but their relationship had been plagued by tragedy and betrayal.

"These letters... they're filled with so much pain and anger," Grace said, her voice trembling as she read the heartbreaking words. "Eliza's spirit must be the one haunting the mansion."

Daniel nodded, his expression grim. "We need to find out what happened to her and Samuel. If we can understand their story, maybe we can find a way to bring her peace."

Meanwhile, Emily stayed by Margaret's side, comforting her and providing support. One evening, as they sat together in the dimly lit living room, Margaret's eyes grew distant.

"Emily, there's something I need to tell you," Margaret said softly. "Something about our family's history."

Emily leaned in, her heart pounding. "What is it, Aunt Margaret?"

Margaret took a deep breath, her eyes filled with a mix of sadness and resolve. "Our family is connected to the mansion. Your great-grandmother was involved in the rituals that were performed there. She tried to stop the darkness, but she failed. That's why the spirit is so strong."

Emily felt a chill run down her spine. "So our family is tied to the mansion's curse?"

Margaret nodded, tears streaming down her face. "Yes, and it's up to you to break the cycle. You have the strength and love to do it, Emily. You can bring peace to the mansion and our family."

With renewed determination, Emily hugged her aunt tightly. "I'll do it, Aunt Margaret. I promise."

Back at the mansion, the situation grew more dire. The spirit's fury was unleashed in full force, with objects flying through the air and a cold, oppressive presence settling over the house. Daniel, Jack, and Grace knew they were running out of time.

"We have to find a way to communicate with Eliza's spirit," Jack said urgently. "If we can understand what she wants, we might be able to help her move on."

Grace nodded, her face pale but determined. "We need to perform a séance. It's risky, but it might be our only chance."

Daniel agreed, his mind racing with the possibilities. "Let's do it. We'll need to prepare everything carefully and make sure we're ready for whatever happens."

As they gathered the necessary items and prepared the grand hall for the séance, the tension in the mansion was palpable. The residents stayed in their rooms, fearful of the spirit's wrath, but hopeful that Daniel, Jack, and Grace could find a solution.

That night, as the clock struck midnight, they began the séance. The room was filled with the soft glow of candlelight, and a chill hung in the air. Grace led the ritual, her voice steady and clear as she called upon Eliza's spirit.

"We seek to understand your pain, Eliza," Grace intoned. "We want to help you find peace."

The air grew colder, and the candles flickered as a ghostly figure appeared in the center of the circle. Eliza's spirit was beautiful yet sorrowful, her eyes filled with a deep, haunting sadness.

"What do you want?" Jack asked gently. "How can we help you?"

Eliza's voice was a whisper, filled with longing and despair. "I was betrayed... my love was taken from me... I seek justice."

Daniel stepped forward, his heart aching for the tormented spirit. "We will help you, Eliza. Tell us what we need to do."

Eliza's form flickered, her voice growing stronger. "Find the truth... bring my story to light... only then will I find peace."

As the séance continued, Eliza revealed more about her tragic past and the betrayal that had led to her death. Daniel, Jack, and Grace listened intently, determined to fulfill her wishes and bring an end to the mansion's curse.

Meanwhile, Emily spent her days caring for Margaret and reflecting on the revelations about her family's connection to the mansion. She knew that her return would be crucial to resolving the situation, but she also understood the importance of being there for her aunt.

In the quiet moments by Margaret's bedside, Emily found strength in her love for Daniel and the support of her friends. She knew that together, they could overcome the darkness and restore peace to the mansion.

As the days passed, the team at the mansion made significant progress in uncovering the truth about Eliza's story. They found hidden letters and artifacts that revealed the depth of her betrayal and the pain that had bound her spirit to the mansion.

With this newfound knowledge, they prepared for the final ritual that would bring justice to Eliza and release her spirit. They knew it would be a difficult and dangerous task, but they were ready to face it head-on.

In the heart of the mansion, amidst the swirling shadows and the echoes of the past, they stood united in their resolve. The spirit's wrath had tested their strength, but their love and determination would guide them through the darkness.

And as Emily prepared to return to the mansion, she knew that her journey was far from over. Together with Daniel, Jack, and Grace, she would face the ultimate challenge and bring light to the shadows that had haunted their lives for so long.

Chapter 7: Unraveling the Mystery

T he mansion stood as a beacon of history and mystery, its walls echoing with stories untold. As the days turned into weeks, the oppressive presence of the spirit grew stronger, making the air thick with tension. Emily's absence left a void, but Daniel, Grace, and Jack were determined to push forward in their quest to uncover the mansion's dark past and find a way to cleanse it.

Grace proved to be an invaluable ally, her knowledge of the mansion's history and her intuitive sense guiding their every step. She took on the responsibility of caring for Daniel, ensuring he was well-supported during Emily's absence. One afternoon,

Daniel sat naked in the hot tub, the water was perfect. The bubbles massaged his back and his legs. He closed his eyes and thought about Emily. He could feel his dick getting hard just thinking about her tight little pussy. He opened his eyes and took hold of his dick. He started slowly stroking it, up and down, imagining it was Emily's mouth. He decided to stop and go back to get ready for the meeting with the Mayor.

Daniel descended the pool stairs, he slipped and fell, grimacing in pain as he clutched his leg. Daniel tried to steady himself but it was too late. He fell backwards, right out of the hot tub. He landed on his back with a loud thud. Daniel's dick was still hard, and it was sticking straight up in the air.

Grace was in the other room, cleaning. She heard the loud thud and came running. She opened the door and saw Daniel lying there, naked and with a hard on. Grace couldn't help but stare at Daniel's dick. It was big and thick, just like she liked it. She couldn't believe how lucky she was.

"Sir, are you okay?" Grace asked as she ran over to him.

"Yeah, I'm fine." Daniel replied, still trying to catch his breath.

Grace helped him to a nearby lounge chair, her touch gentle yet firm. "Let me take a look." She carefully examined his ankle, her fingers skillfully assessing the damage. "It's swollen. We need to get some ice and ointment."

As she tended to his injury, applying a soothing ointment and wrapping his ankle with care, Daniel felt a deep gratitude. "Thank you, Grace. I don't know what I'd do without you."

Grace smiled softly, her eyes warm. "It's my pleasure, Sir."

Grace offered Daniel a towel, but as she handed it to him, she couldn't help but notice how hard his dick still was. She couldn't resist the temptation any longer. She reached out and touched it. Daniel flinched, but he didn't say anything.

"Sir, I've wanted to do this for so long." Grace said as she started stroking his dick.

Daniel didn't know what to do. He was devoted to Emily, but he couldn't deny the fact that Grace's touch felt good. He closed his eyes and let her continue. Grace started to get more aggressive, she was moaning and breathing heavily. Daniel couldn't take it anymore, he opened his eyes and looked at Grace.

"Grace, we can't do this." Daniel said as he pushed her hand away.

Grace was disappointed, but she understood and had to obey her Master. She got up, apolgized and left the room, leaving Daniel alone with his thoughts. Daniel sat there for a few minutes, trying to clear his head. He couldn't believe what had just happened. He got up and put on his robe, he was still hard, but he knew he had to take care of it himself.

Daniel went back to his room and locked the door. He sat on the bed and started stroking his dick again. He thought about Grace and Emily, her touch, her moans. He couldn't help but imagine what it would be like to fuck her. He closed his eyes and imagined Grace on her knees, sucking his dick and Emily watching from the bed. He started stroking faster and faster, until he finally cum.

Daniel lay there for a few minutes, trying to catch his breath. He couldn't believe what had just happened. He had just cheated on Emily, with the maid. He knew he had to tell her, but he didn't know how. He got up and got dressed.

The bond between them, Daniel and Grace grew stronger with each passing day, built on mutual respect and shared determination. Grace's unwavering support gave Daniel the strength to continue their search, even in Emily's absence.

Meanwhile, miles away, Emily sat by her aunt Margaret's bedside, providing comfort and companionship. Margaret's health had slowly begun to improve, her spirits lifted by Emily's presence and their heartfelt conversations.

"Emily, you have a special kind of strength," Margaret said one evening, her voice a soft murmur. "I know you'll bring peace to that mansion."

Emily squeezed her aunt's hand, her eyes filled with resolve. "I'll do everything I can, Aunt Margaret. For you, for our family, and for everyone at the mansion."

With Margaret's health stabilizing, Emily knew it was time to return home. She packed her bags with a renewed sense of purpose, determined to bring an end to the spirit's torment. She hugged Margaret tightly, promising to visit again soon.

"Be safe, my dear," Margaret whispered. "And remember, love is your greatest strength."

Emily's journey back to the mansion was filled with anticipation and a touch of anxiety. She couldn't wait to be reunited with Daniel and her friends, eager to continue their mission together. When she finally arrived, the mansion's grand facade loomed before her, a mix of beauty and foreboding.

Daniel met her at the entrance, his face lighting up with relief and joy. "Emily, thank God you're back."

Emily embraced him, feeling the familiar warmth of his arms around her. "I missed you so much, Daniel. How's everything here?"

He kissed her forehead, his voice filled with affection. "We missed you too. Things have been intense, but we're making progress. Grace and Jack have been amazing."

As they walked inside, Emily saw Grace and Jack waiting in the library, their faces reflecting the weariness of their efforts but also the hope of their discoveries. Grace stood up, her eyes brightening at the sight of Emily.

"Welcome back, Emily. We have so much to tell you."

They gathered around the table, where maps, letters, and ancient texts were spread out in an organized chaos. Grace began to recount their findings, her voice steady and filled with determination.

"We've uncovered more about Eliza and Samuel's story. It turns out, Eliza's spirit was bound to the mansion by a powerful ritual gone wrong. She believed Samuel betrayed her, but it was actually a jealous rival who cursed them both."

Emily listened intently, her mind racing with the implications. "So, to free Eliza's spirit, we need to break the curse and reveal the truth to her."

Jack nodded. "Exactly. We need to perform a final ritual to cleanse the mansion and set Eliza free. But it won't be easy. The spirit is growing more powerful, and we'll need to be prepared for anything."

Daniel squeezed Emily's hand, his eyes reflecting his unwavering support. "We'll do it together. We've come this far, and we won't back down now."

Over the next few days, they meticulously planned the final ritual, gathering the necessary items and creating a sacred space in the grand hall. Emily felt a renewed sense of purpose, her heart filled with love and determination. She knew that with Daniel, Grace, and Jack by her side, they could overcome any obstacle.

On the night of the ritual, the mansion was eerily silent. The air was thick with anticipation as they gathered in the grand hall, surrounded by candles and ancient artifacts. The atmosphere was charged with a mix of fear and hope, the weight of their mission pressing down on them.

Grace began the incantations, her voice steady and clear as she called upon the spirits and invoked the ancient rites. The air grew colder, and a palpable tension filled the room. The spirit's presence was strong, its anger and sorrow palpable.

"We seek to end your suffering, Eliza," Grace intoned. "We seek to bring you peace."

As the ritual progressed, the spirit's form began to materialize, a ghostly figure filled with anguish and longing. Emily stepped forward, her voice filled with compassion and resolve.

"Eliza, we know the truth. Samuel never betrayed you. It was a rival who cursed you both. Let us help you find peace."

Eliza's spirit wavered, her eyes filled with a mixture of sadness and hope. "The pain... the betrayal..."

Emily reached out, her hand hovering just above the spirit's form. "Let go of the past, Eliza. Trust us. We will bring justice to your story."

The room seemed to tremble as the final words of the ritual echoed through the hall. The spirit's form began to dissipate, the anger and sorrow slowly giving way to a sense of release. As the spirit faded, a calmness settled over the mansion, the oppressive presence lifting.

Emily turned to Daniel, her eyes filled with tears of relief and joy. "We did it, Daniel. We brought her peace."

Daniel pulled her into a tight embrace, his voice filled with love and pride. "Yes, we did. Together."

Grace and Jack joined them, their faces reflecting the triumph of their efforts. "This is just the beginning," Grace said, her voice filled with hope. "The mansion is finally free from its past, and we can create a new future."

Emily smiled, feeling a deep sense of peace. "And we'll do it together, as a community. This place will be a beacon of love and light."

As they stood together, bathed in the warm glow of the candles, Emily knew that their journey was far from over. But with Daniel by her side and the strength of their love, they could face any challenge that came their way.

The mystery had been unraveled, and the shadows had been banished. The mansion was once again a place of hope and beauty, a testament to the power of love and unity. And as Emily looked around at the faces of her friends and neighbors, she knew that their story was only just beginning.

Chapter 8: Blossoming Love

The mansion, now a place of determination and hope, was also becoming the backdrop for a budding romance. Amidst the chaos and supernatural disturbances, Jack and Grace found themselves drawn to each other in ways they had never expected. Their connection grew stronger with each passing day, providing a source of comfort and strength for both of them.

Grace had always admired Jack's dedication and intelligence. His calm demeanor and deep knowledge of the mansion's history had been invaluable in their quest to uncover the truth. Jack, in turn, found himself captivated by Grace's beauty, resilience, and quiet strength. She was not just a maid; she was a beacon of light in the darkness that enveloped the mansion.

One evening, as the sun set and the mansion was bathed in the golden glow of twilight, Jack found Grace in the garden, tending to the flowers. The garden had become her sanctuary, a place where she could find solace and peace amidst the turmoil.

"Grace," Jack called softly, not wanting to startle her.

She looked up, her eyes lighting up at the sight of him. "Jack, I didn't hear you come in. Is everything alright?"

He smiled, his heart warming at her concern. "Everything's fine. I just needed a break and thought I'd find you here."

Grace wiped her hands on her apron and stood up, her face radiating a gentle beauty that took Jack's breath away. "It's been a long day. The garden helps me clear my mind."

Jack nodded, stepping closer. "I can see why. It's beautiful here, just like you."

Grace blushed, looking away shyly. "Thank you, Jack. That means a lot."

They stood in comfortable silence for a moment, the sounds of the garden and the distant chirping of birds creating a serene atmosphere. Jack took a deep breath, feeling the weight of his emotions. "Grace, I know things have been chaotic, but I've come to realize how much you mean to me. Your strength, your kindness... you've been my rock through all of this."

Grace's eyes met his, filled with a mixture of surprise and emotion. "Jack, I feel the same way. You've been a constant source of support and courage. I don't know what I would have done without you."

Jack took her hand, his touch gentle and reassuring. "Grace, I care about you deeply. And I want to be there for you, not just as a friend, but as someone who loves you."

Tears welled up in Grace's eyes as she smiled. "I love you too, Jack. More than I ever thought possible."

Their words hung in the air, a promise of a new beginning. Jack pulled Grace into a tender embrace, their hearts beating in unison. The garden, with its blooming flowers and fragrant scents, seemed to envelop them in a cocoon of love and warmth.

Grace looked into Jack's eyes, feeling her heart race with anticipation. The sun was setting, casting a warm glow over the garden, and the scent of blooming flowers filled the air. She could feel her pussy tingling with desire from what he saw earlier with Daniel, knowing that soon she would be in Jack's arms, feeling his strong body pressed against hers.

"I want you, Jack," she whispered, her voice barely above a whisper.

Jack's eyes darkened with lust as he pulled Grace closer, his hands roaming over her curves. He could feel the heat radiating from her body, and he knew that she wanted him just as much as he wanted her.

"I've wanted you for so long, Grace," he murmured, his lips brushing against her ear.

Grace shivered with pleasure as Jack's hands slid under her dress, cupping her ass and pulling her closer. She could feel his hard cock pressing against her, and she knew that she had to have him.

"Oh..Jack" she begged, her voice husky with desire.

Jack didn't need any more encouragement. He quickly stripped off Grace's dress, leaving her standing naked. She was not wearing any bra or panties. He took a moment to admire her body, his eyes roaming over her curves and taking in every inch of her.

"You're so fucking beautiful, Grace," he said, his voice filled with awe and lust.

Grace blushed at the compliment, but she didn't have time to respond. Jack was already on his knees, his mouth pressed against her panties. She could feel his tongue flicking against her clit, and she moaned with pleasure.

"Oh, fuck, Jack," she gasped, her hands tangling in his hair.

Jack continued to lick and suck on Grace's clit, his fingers sliding into her pussy. She was so wet, so ready for him, and he couldn't wait to be inside her.

"I need you, Jack," Grace begged, her voice filled with desperation.

Jack stood up, his cock straining against his pants. He quickly undid his pants, freeing his hard dick. He couldn't wait any longer. He had to have Grace.

He pushed her down onto the grass, spreading her legs wide. He positioned himself at her entrance, teasing her with his cock.

"Please, Jack," Grace begged, her hips bucking up towards him.

Jack finally gave in, sliding his cock inside her. He groaned with pleasure as he felt her tight pussy wrapped around him. He started to thrust, hard and deep, his balls slapping against her ass.

Grace moaned with pleasure, her nails digging into Jack's back. She could feel her orgasm building, her pussy clenching around Jack's cock.

"I'm going to cum, Jack," she gasped, her hips bucking up to meet his thrusts.

Jack could feel Grace's pussy tightening around his cock, and he knew that she was close. He thrust harder and deeper, his balls tightening as he felt his own orgasm building.

"Cum for me, Grace," he growled, his hips pistoning faster.

Grace cried out as she came, her pussy clenching around Jack's cock. He groaned as he felt her cum, his own orgasm crashing over him. He pulled out and cum on Graces belly button and pussy, giving her a deep kiss on lips.

They lay there, panting and gasping for breath, their bodies slick with sweat.

"I love you, Grace, can we do it again tonight" he whispered, his lips brushing against her ear.

Grace smiled, her fingers tracing patterns on Jack's chest.

"We can if the weather permits, it might rain" she whispered back.

Their words hung in the air, a promise of a new beginning. The garden, with its blooming flowers and fragrant scents, seemed to envelop them in a cocoon of love and warmth. They knew that they had a long road ahead of them, but they were ready to face it together. And as they lay there, wrapped in each other's arms, they knew that they would always have this moment, this perfect moment, to look back on.

As the days went by, their bond only grew stronger. They worked side by side, their love providing a beacon of hope amidst the darkness. Jack's unwavering support gave Grace the strength to face each new challenge, while Grace's gentle presence grounded Jack and reminded him of the beauty in life.

Their relationship did not go unnoticed by Emily and Daniel, who were delighted to see them finding happiness amidst the turmoil. One evening, as they all gathered in the grand hall to discuss their next steps, Emily couldn't help but smile at the sight of Jack and Grace sitting close together, their hands intertwined.

"You two make a wonderful team," Emily said, her voice filled with warmth. Grace blushed, but her eyes shone with happiness. "Thank you, Emily. We've found strength in each other, just as you and Daniel have."

Daniel nodded, his expression thoughtful. "Love has a way of giving us the courage to face even the darkest of times. And together, we can overcome anything."

With their love as a foundation, Jack and Grace threw themselves into the task of uncovering more about the mansion's dark history. They spent long hours in the library, poring over old documents and artifacts, piecing together the final ritual needed to cleanse the mansion.

One night, as they worked late into the evening, Grace found an old diary hidden among the stacks of books. The diary belonged to Eliza, the tormented spirit that haunted the mansion. As they read through the pages, they uncovered more details about her tragic love story with Samuel and the betrayal that had led to the curse.

"Eliza's pain is palpable," Grace said softly, her voice filled with empathy. "She loved Samuel deeply, but the curse twisted her feelings into something dark and vengeful."

Jack nodded, his brow furrowed in concentration. "We need to show her the truth. If we can help her see that Samuel never betrayed her, we might be able to free her spirit."

Their determination grew stronger with each revelation, fueled by their love for each other and their commitment to helping Emily and Daniel. Together, they devised a plan to perform the final ritual, gathering the necessary items and creating a sacred space in the grand hall.

As the night of the ritual approached, the atmosphere in the mansion was charged with anticipation. The community members, who had come to respect and admire Jack and Grace, rallied around them, offering their support and encouragement.

On the night of the ritual, the grand hall was filled with the soft glow of candles, the air thick with the scent of incense. Emily, Daniel, Jack, and Grace stood together in the center of the room, their hands joined in a circle.

Grace began the incantations, her voice steady and clear as she called upon the spirits and invoked the ancient rites. The air grew colder, and a palpable tension filled the room. The spirit's presence was strong, its anger and sorrow palpable.

"We seek to end your suffering, Eliza," Grace intoned. "We seek to bring you peace."

As the ritual progressed, the spirit's form began to materialize, a ghostly figure filled with anguish and longing. Emily stepped forward, her voice filled with compassion and resolve.

"Eliza, we know the truth. Samuel never betrayed you. It was a rival who cursed you both. Let us help you find peace."

Eliza's spirit wavered, her eyes filled with a mixture of sadness and hope. "The pain... the betrayal..."

Emily reached out, her hand hovering just above the spirit's form. "Let go of the past, Eliza. Trust us. We will bring justice to your story."

The room seemed to tremble as the final words of the ritual echoed through the hall. The spirit's form began to dissipate, the anger and sorrow slowly giving way to a sense of release. As the spirit faded, a calmness settled over the mansion, the oppressive presence lifting.

Emily turned to Daniel, her eyes filled with tears of relief and joy. "We did it, Daniel. We brought her peace."

Daniel pulled her into a tight embrace, his voice filled with love and pride. "Yes, we did. Together."

Grace and Jack joined them, their faces reflecting the triumph of their efforts. "This is just the beginning," Grace said, her voice filled with hope. "The mansion is finally free from its past, and we can create a new future."

Emily smiled, feeling a deep sense of peace. "And we'll do it together, as a community. This place will be a beacon of love and light."

As they stood together, bathed in the warm glow of the candles, Emily knew that their journey was far from over. But with Daniel by her side and the strength of their love, they could face any challenge that came their way.

The mystery had been unraveled, and the shadows had been banished. The mansion was once again a place of hope and beauty, a testament to the power of love and unity. And as Emily looked around at the faces of her friends and neighbors, she knew that their story was only just beginning.

Chapter 9: The Final Confrontation

The atmosphere in the mansion was thick with anticipation and determination. The time had come for the ultimate confrontation with the malevolent spirit that had haunted the mansion for so long. Emily and Daniel, their love and resolve stronger than ever, knew they had to face this challenge head-on.

The sun had set, casting long shadows across the grand hall where the final battle would take place. The community members, who had grown to love and support Emily and Daniel, gathered around them, offering their encouragement and strength. It was a powerful testament to the unity and hope that had blossomed amidst the mansion's turmoil.

Daniel took Emily's hand, his eyes filled with love and determination. "Emily, there's something I need to share with you before we begin," he said, his voice steady. "It's about what happened with Grace at the pool."

Emily nodded, her expression calm but curious. "What is it, Daniel?"

Daniel took a deep breath, his gaze unwavering. "When you were away, I slipped on the stairs by the pool and hurt my ankle. Grace was there, and she helped me. She took care of me, applied ointment, and made sure I was okay. It was nothing more than that, but I wanted you to know because I don't want any secrets between us."

Emily squeezed his hand, her heart swelling with love and gratitude. "Thank you for telling me, Daniel. I trust you, and I trust Grace. I know that you both only want what's best for us and for the mansion."

Daniel smiled, relief washing over him. "I love you, Emily. More than anything. And together, we can face whatever comes our way."

With their hearts aligned and their resolve firm, Emily and Daniel turned to the gathered community. Jack and Grace stood close by, their expressions reflecting the seriousness of the moment.

"We're all in this together," Jack said, his voice filled with conviction. "The spirit's power is strong, but so is our determination. We've uncovered the truth about Eliza's story, and we know what we need to do to set her free."

Grace nodded, her eyes shining with resolve. "We need to perform the final ritual, but this time, we'll do it right. We'll show Eliza the truth and help her find peace."

As they made their final preparations, the air in the mansion grew colder, a chilling reminder of the spirit's presence. The grand hall was filled with the soft glow of candles, and ancient artifacts were arranged meticulously to create a sacred space.

Emily and Daniel stood at the center of the hall, their hands joined in a circle with Jack and Grace. The community members formed a protective ring around them, their support palpable and unwavering.

Daniel couldn't help but notice how beautiful Grace looked tonight. Her dark hair cascaded down her shoulders, and her green eyes sparkled in the light of the candles on the table. She was wearing a tight-fitting dress that showed off her curves, and Daniel couldn't help but feel a stirring in his pants. Daniel was surprised, but the idea of being with Grace was becoming more and more appealing.

Grace began the incantations, her voice steady and clear as she called upon the spirits and invoked the ancient rites. The air grew heavier, and a palpable tension filled the room. The spirit's presence was almost tangible, its anger and sorrow filling the space.

"We seek to end your suffering, Eliza," Grace intoned, her voice echoing through the hall. "We seek to bring you peace."

Grace looked up at Daniel, her eyes wide with surprise. She didn't know what to say, but she couldn't deny the feelings that were stirring inside Daniel and lust she was now seeing in his eyes.

As the ritual progressed, the spirit's form began to materialize, a ghostly figure filled with anguish and longing. Emily stepped forward, her voice filled with compassion and resolve.

"Eliza, we know the truth. Samuel never betrayed you. It was a rival who cursed you both. Let us help you find peace."

Eliza's spirit wavered, her eyes filled with a mixture of sadness and hope. "The pain... the betrayal..."

Emily reached out, her hand hovering just above the spirit's form. "Let go of the past, Eliza. Trust us. We will bring justice to your story."

The room seemed to tremble as the final words of the ritual echoed through the hall. The spirit's form began to dissipate, the anger and sorrow slowly giving way to a sense of release. As the spirit faded, a calmness settled over the mansion, the oppressive presence lifting.

But just as they thought it was over, a sudden gust of wind swept through the hall, extinguishing the candles. The spirit reappeared, its form more menacing and powerful than before. It was clear that the final confrontation was not yet over.

Daniel tightened his grip on Emily's hand, his voice filled with determination. "We won't give up. We will bring you peace, Eliza."

Grace continued the incantations, her voice unwavering. "Eliza, listen to us. You deserve to rest. You deserve peace."

The spirit's form flickered, its anger and sorrow battling against the truth that Emily, Daniel, Jack, and Grace were trying to convey. The room was filled with a swirling energy, a battle between light and darkness.

In a moment of clarity, Emily stepped forward, her voice filled with love and compassion. "Eliza, remember the love you had for Samuel. Remember the happiness you shared. That love is stronger than any curse. Let it guide you to peace."

Eliza's spirit paused, her eyes locking onto Emily's. The room fell silent, the tension palpable. Slowly, the spirit's form began to soften, the anger and sorrow giving way to a sense of acceptance.

"Eliza, trust us," Daniel said, his voice gentle but firm. "We will help you find peace."

With one final, haunting wail, the spirit began to dissolve, the anger and sorrow melting away. The room was filled with a soft, warm light, a sense of peace and tranquility washing over everyone.

As the spirit faded completely, the candles relit, their flames dancing gently. The oppressive presence was gone, replaced by a sense of calm and serenity. The mansion, once filled with darkness and turmoil, was now a place of hope and light.

Emily turned to Daniel, tears of relief and joy streaming down her face. "We did it, Daniel. We brought her peace."

Daniel pulled her into a tight embrace, his voice filled with love and pride and looking at Grace from the side of his eye, her voluptuous body, which he never noticed earlier. "Yes, we did. Together."

The community erupted into applause, their cheers echoing through the grand hall. Jack and Grace joined Emily and Daniel, their faces reflecting the triumph of their efforts.

"This is just the beginning," Grace said, her voice filled with hope. "The mansion is finally free from its past, and we can create a new future."

Emily smiled, feeling a deep sense of peace. "And we'll do it together, as a community. This place will be a beacon of love and light."

As they stood together, bathed in the warm glow of the candles, Emily knew that their journey was far from over. But with Daniel by her side and the strength of their love, they could face any challenge that came their way.

The mystery had been unraveled, and the shadows had been banished. The mansion was once again a place of hope and beauty, a testament to the power of love and unity. And as Emily looked around at the faces of her friends and neighbors, she knew that their story was only just beginning. Daniel had other thoughts in his mind about Grace.

Chapter 10: The Ultimate Sacrifice

The mansion's grand hall was filled with an eerie stillness, the calm before the storm. Candles flickered, casting long shadows on the walls, and the ancient artifacts seemed to hum with a mysterious energy. Emily and Daniel stood at the center, their hands tightly clasped, their hearts pounding with anticipation and fear. They knew that that night would be their ultimate test, a final confrontation that would require everything they had to give.

Jack and Grace stood nearby; their faces set with determination. They had become more than just allies; we were united by a common purpose. The community members, who had gathered to support them, formed a protective circle around the four, their presence a silent promise of solidarity.

Grace began to chant, her voice steady and filled with power. The air grew colder, and a palpable tension filled the room. The spirit's presence was almost tangible, a dark force that seemed to press down on everyone. Emily and Daniel exchanged a glance, drawing strength from each other.

"We can do this," Daniel whispered, his voice filled with conviction. "Together."

Daniel had eyes only for Grace. Her voluptuous body was accentuated by her tight red dress. Her sexy lips moved gracefully as she continued her chants. Daniel stole a glance at her breasts. The tight red dress revealed her cleavage. He could see the outline of her nipples through the thin fabric. He imagined her naked, her big tits bouncing up and down as he fucked her hard. He imagined her moaning in pleasure as he licked her nipples and sucked them into his mouth. He imagined her pussy getting wetter and wetter as he explored her body with his tongue. Grace knew Daniel was looking at her body, but she continued with her chants and ignored the gaze.

Daniel shifted in his focus, trying to hide his growing erection. He glanced at Emily, his wife, but she was too engrossed in the recital to notice.

Emily nodded and smiled, her eyes shining with love and resolve. "Together."

As Grace's incantations grew louder, the spirit began to materialize, a ghostly figure filled with anger and sorrow. Eliza's form wavered, her eyes burning with a mix of pain and desperation.

"You betrayed me," Eliza's voice echoed through the hall, filled with a haunting rage. "You took everything from me."

Emily stepped forward; her voice gentle but firm. "Eliza, we know the truth. It wasn't Samuel who betrayed you. It was a rival who cursed you both. We're here to set you free."

The spirit recoiled, her form flickering as if caught between two worlds. "Lies... all lies..."

Daniel tightened his grip on Emily's hand. "We have the proof, Eliza. We found the letters, the diary. Samuel loved you deeply. He would never have betrayed you."

Eliza's eyes softened for a moment, a flicker of hope passing through them. But the darkness was strong, and her anger surged again. "I can't... I can't let go..."

Grace stepped forward; her voice filled with compassion. "Eliza, it's time to let go of the past. Your love for Samuel can guide you to peace. Trust us."

The spirit's form wavered, torn between the pain of the past and the promise of peace. Emily felt a surge of determination. They needed to do more. They needed to show Eliza the truth in a way that would break through the darkness.

"There's one more thing we need to do," Emily said, her voice trembling with the weight of the decision. "We need to perform the final ritual, but it will require a great sacrifice."

Daniel looked at her, his eyes filled with love and understanding. "Whatever it takes, Emily. I'm with you."

Emily turned to Grace and Jack, her heart aching with the enormity of what they were about to do. "We need your help. This ritual... it will bind our spirits together with Eliza's, just long enough to show her the truth. But it will leave us vulnerable."

Jack's face was resolute. "We'll protect you. Whatever it takes."

Grace nodded, her eyes shining with tears. "We're with you, Emily. Always."

With the support of their friends, Emily and Daniel prepared for the final ritual. They placed candles in a circle around them, each one representing a part of the past, present, and future. The ancient artifacts were arranged carefully, their power amplifying the ritual's energy.

As they stood at the center of the circle, Emily felt a deep sense of calm wash over her. She looked into Daniel's eyes, drawing strength from their love. "Are you ready?"

Daniel smiled; his eyes filled with unwavering devotion. "With you, always."

Grace began the final incantation, her voice resonating with power. The air grew thick with energy, and the spirit's form became more defined, her eyes locked onto Emily and Daniel. Daniel smiled and continued his gaze of lust for Grace.

As the ritual progressed, Emily felt a strange sensation, as if her spirit was reaching out, connecting with Eliza's. She could feel the depth of Eliza's pain, the betrayal that had consumed her. But she also felt the love that had once filled Eliza's heart, a love so powerful it could transcend time.

"Eliza," Emily whispered, her voice filled with emotion. "Feel the love you had for Samuel. Let it guide you."

The spirit's form flickered, her eyes softening. "Samuel... I loved him so much..."

Daniel's voice joined Emily's, strong and filled with compassion. "He loved you too, Eliza. He never betrayed you. Let us show you the truth."

The room seemed to pulse with energy as the ritual reached its climax. Emily and Daniel's spirits intertwined with Eliza's, their love creating a bridge to the past. In that moment, the truth was revealed. Eliza saw the betrayal for what it was, a dark curse cast by a jealous rival. She saw Samuel's unwavering love, his heartbreak at being unable to protect her.

Tears streamed down Eliza's ghostly face, her anger dissolving into sorrow and acceptance. "I see it now... the truth... Samuel... I..."

Emily felt a surge of relief as Eliza's spirit began to fade, her form becoming more peaceful. "Find peace, Eliza. Your love will guide you."

With a final, haunting whisper, Eliza's spirit dissipated, the darkness lifting from the mansion. The candles burned brighter, their flames a symbol of hope and renewal.

Emily turned to Daniel, tears of joy and relief in her eyes. "We did it, Daniel. We set her free."

Daniel pulled her into a tight embrace, his voice filled with love and pride. "Yes, we did. Together."

Grace and Jack joined them in the group hug and Daniel felt tender breasts of Grace touching his elbow giving him an instant erection, their faces reflecting the triumph and relief of their efforts. "This is a new beginning," Grace said, her voice filled with hope. "The mansion is free, and we can create a future filled with love and light."

Emily smiled, feeling a deep sense of peace and fulfillment. "And we'll do it together, as a community. This place will be a beacon of hope and unity."

As they stood together, bathed in the warm glow of the candles, Emily knew that their journey was far from over. But with Daniel by her side and the strength of their love, they could face any challenge that came their way.

The ultimate sacrifice had been made, but it was a testament to the power of love and unity. The mansion, once a place of darkness and sorrow, was now a symbol of hope and renewal. And as Emily looked around at the faces of her friends and neighbors, she knew that their story was only just beginning.

Jack had a hard on from energy of the ritual and wanted to have Grace now and nudged her secretly to come to the garden room. Daniel overheard the conversation.

Grace walked into the garden house, her heart pounding as she thought about what was about to happen. She was nervous, but excited at the same time. She had always found Jack to be attractive and last few times they made love he was good too. She had caught him looking at her a few times today, and she knew that he wanted her just as much as she wanted him.

As she entered the garden house, she saw Jack sitting on a couch, his muscular body on full display. He was naked, his cock already hard and ready for her. She felt her pussy getting wet just looking at him, and she knew that she was in for a treat.

"Come here, Grace," Jack said, his voice deep and commanding. She walked over to him, her heart racing as she stood in front of him. He reached out and touched her cheek, his fingers tracing her lips. "You have such beautiful lips," he said, his eyes filled with desire.

She felt her pussy getting even wetter as he leaned in and kissed her. His lips were soft and warm, and she could feel his cock pressing against her belly. She reached down and wrapped her hand around it, feeling its heat and hardness. He moaned as she started to stroke him, his hips thrusting forward as he fucked her hand.

"I want you, Grace," he said, his voice husky with desire. "I want to fuck you so hard. After freeing the spirits, I am feeling a sudden increase in desire."

She nodded, unable to speak as he stood up and led her to the bed. He pushed her down onto it, his body covering hers as he kissed her again. She could feel his cock pressing against her pussy, and she spread her legs wider, inviting him in.

He entered her slowly, his cock filling her up as he started to thrust. She wrapped her legs around him, pulling him deeper inside her. He fucked her hard and fast, his hips slapping against hers as he pounded into her. She could feel herself getting close to orgasm, her pussy clenching around his cock as she moaned with pleasure.

"Fuck, Grace," he groaned, his thrusts becoming erratic as he came. She could feel his hot cum filling her up, and she moaned as she came too, her orgasm ripping through her.

They lay there for a moment, panting and sweating as they caught their breath. Jack looked down at her, his eyes filled with satisfaction. "You're amazing, Grace," he said, his voice soft. Just then Jack received a phone call from the Mayor and the Mayor was in the library and wanted to discuss the funding for next year. Jack had to leave urgently. He kissed Grace and apologized for the rush.

She smiled, feeling happy and content.

As she lay there naked, eyes closed and thinking about Jack, she heard the door open, and Daniel walked in. He had watched the whole thing, his cock hard in his pants. He walked over to the bed, his eyes fixed on Grace's pussy, still wet with Jack's cum.

"I want a turn," he said, his voice husky.

Grace looked at him, her eyes filled with desire. She knew that she wanted him too, and she used her skirt to clean Jacks cum, she spread her legs wider, inviting him in. He climbed onto the bed, his cock hard and ready. He entered her slowly, his cock filling her up as he started to thrust. She wrapped her legs around him, pulling him deeper inside her. He fucked her hard and fast, his hips slapping against hers as he pounded into her. She could feel herself getting close to orgasm again, her pussy clenching around his cock as she moaned with pleasure.

"Fuck, Grace," he groaned, his thrusts becoming erratic as he came. She could feel his hot cum filling her up, and she moaned as she came too, her orgasm ripping through her.

They lay there for a moment, panting and sweating as they caught their breath. Grace looked at him, her eyes filled with satisfaction. She had never felt this way before, and she knew that she would never forget this moment. She knew that she would always remember the way Jack and Daniel had made her feel, the way they had made her body sing with pleasure today.

As they lay there, they heard footsteps. Daniel knew it was Emily. Daniel and Grace immediately got up, picked up the dresses and ran for the other door. They hide behind the back door. The front Door opens again, and this time, it was Emily.

Grace looked at Emily from behind the door as Daniel continued feeling her from behind, she felt Emily's eyes are filled with desire and is looking for Daniel.

Chapter 11: Healing and Celebration

The grand hall, once the site of so much pain and turmoil, was now a place of joy and celebration. The air was filled with laughter and the soft murmur of conversation as the community gathered to celebrate their victory over the malevolent spirit. Candles flickered warmly, casting a golden glow over the room, and the scent of fresh flowers filled the air, a testament to the renewal and hope that had taken root in the mansion.

Emily and Daniel stood at the center of the hall, their hands intertwined, their hearts brimming with happiness and relief. They had faced the darkness together, and their love had emerged stronger and more resilient than ever. The trials they had endured had only deepened their bond, solidifying their commitment to each other and to the future they were building together.

As the celebration continued around them, Emily looked up at Daniel, her eyes shining with love. "I can't believe how far we've come," she said softly, her voice filled with wonder. "We've been through so much, but here we are, surrounded by our friends and our community, stronger than ever."

Daniel smiled, his gaze filled with affection and pride. "We did it together, Emily. Your strength, your courage—they've been my guiding light through all of this. I love you more than words can express."

Emily felt tears of happiness welling up in her eyes. "I love you too, Daniel. More than anything."

Their moment was interrupted by Jack and Grace, who approached with wide smiles and glasses of champagne. "To the heroes of the mansion!" Jack declared, raising his glass in a toast. "You two have shown us all what true love and determination look like."

Grace nodded, her eyes sparkling with happiness. "And you've given us hope and a future. We're so grateful to have you in our lives." Daniel looked at Grace, she was looking beautiful.

Emily and Daniel clinked their glasses with Jack and Grace, the sound of laughter and celebration filling the hall. As they sipped their champagne, Emily noticed the way Jack and Grace looked at each other, their eyes filled with a deep and abiding love.

"You two are pretty incredible yourselves," Emily said, smiling at them. "Your love and support have been a beacon for all of us."

Jack blushed, glancing at Grace with a tender expression. "We've been through a lot, but I can't imagine doing it with anyone else."

Grace leaned into him; her smile radiant. "Jack has been my rock, and our love has only grown stronger through all of this."

The four of them stood together, basking in the warmth of their friendship and the love that had brought them through the darkness. The community members mingled around them, sharing stories and laughter, the bonds forged through their shared experiences evident in every interaction.

As the evening progressed, the celebration moved to the mansion's garden, now a place of beauty and tranquility. The flowers that Grace and Jack had lovingly tended were in full bloom, their vibrant colors a symbol of the renewal and hope that had taken root in the mansion.

Under the soft light of the moon, Emily and Daniel found a quiet moment together, sitting on a bench and gazing out at the garden. The sounds of the celebration continued in the background, a joyful symphony of voices and laughter.

"This garden is so beautiful," Emily said, her voice filled with awe. "It's a testament to the love and care that we've all put into this place."

Daniel wrapped his arm around her, pulling her close. "It's a reflection of what we've built together. Our love, our community—it's all right here."

Emily rested her head on his shoulder, feeling a profound sense of peace and contentment. "We've come so far, Daniel. And I know that whatever the future holds, we'll face it together."

Daniel kissed the top of her head, his heart filled with love. "Always, Emily. Always."

As they sat together, surrounded by the beauty of the garden and the sounds of celebration, Emily felt a deep sense of gratitude. The mansion, once a place of darkness and sorrow, was now a beacon of hope and love. The trials they had faced had only strengthened their bond, and their love had emerged stronger and more resilient than ever.

SUDDENLY, DANIEL GRABBED Emily's hand and led her to the garden room. It was dimly lit, with a few candles flickering on the tables. The sound of laughter and music could be heard in the background celebrations. Daniel closed the door behind them and pulled Emily towards him. He wrapped his arms around her and kissed her passionately, his tongue exploring her mouth. Emily responded eagerly, her hands running through his hair.

Daniel pulled down his pants, revealing his hard dick. Emily looked at it with desire and grabbed it with her hand. She started to stroke it, causing Daniel to moan. Emily then took it in her mouth and started to suck it, her tongue swirling around the tip. Daniel's moans became louder as Emily's head bobbed up and down.

He lifted her skirt, spread her legs and started to fuck her, hard. Emily's moans filled the room as Daniel's dick slammed into her pussy. Daniel couldn't help but to think about Grace, the girl he had fucked yesterday at the same spot. He imagined it was her pussy he was fucking, and it made him even harder. Emily's moans became louder as Daniel's thrusts became faster.

"Fuck, Daniel, I'm gonna cum, you are too strong and rough today." Emily screamed as Daniel's dick hit her g-spot. Daniel could feel Emily's pussy clenching around his dick as she came. Daniel's orgasm hit him like a truck, and he filled Emily's pussy with his cum. They both lay there, panting and satisfied.

"Wow, Daniel, where did that come from. Spirits?" Emily whispered, as she kissed him. Daniel smiled and replied, "Yeah, spirits probably, Emily. I love you." They both got dressed and went back to the living room, where everyone was still celebrating. But Daniel and Emily had their own secret celebration in the garden room, a celebration that they would never forget.

During the celebration, Jack and Grace found a moment of their own, standing together near a blooming rose bush. Jack took Grace's hand, his eyes filled with emotion. "Grace, these past few months have been some of the most challenging of my life, but they've also been the most rewarding. You've been my anchor, my source of strength."

Grace smiled, tears of happiness in her eyes. "And you've been mine, Jack. I can't imagine going through this without you. I love you more than I ever thought possible."

Jack pulled her into a gentle embrace, their hearts beating in unison. "I love you too, Grace. More than words can say."

As they held each other, the garden around them seemed to glow with the warmth of their love. The community, united by their shared experiences and the bonds they had forged, continued to celebrate, their hearts filled with joy and hope for the future.

Emily and Daniel, along with Jack and Grace, knew that their journey was far from over. But they also knew that they were not alone. With their love and the support of their community, they could face any challenge that came their way. The mansion, once a place of darkness and sorrow, was now a symbol of hope and renewal, a testament to the power of love and unity.

As the night wore on and the celebration continued, Emily and Daniel looked around at the faces of their friends and neighbors, feeling a deep sense of gratitude and fulfillment. Their story was one of love, resilience, and hope—a story that was only just beginning.

Chapter 12: New Beginnings

The morning sun filtered through the large, ornate windows of the mansion, casting a warm and golden light over the grand hall. The echoes of the previous night's celebration still lingered in the air, a testament to the joy and unity that had filled the room. Emily and Daniel stood together, their hands intertwined, gazing out at the beautiful garden that lay beyond the windows.

The mansion, once a place of darkness and sorrow, had been transformed into a beacon of light and love. The journey had been long and arduous, filled with challenges and heartache, but it had also brought them closer together, forging unbreakable bonds of friendship and love.

Emily sighed contentedly, resting her head on Daniel's shoulder. "Can you believe how far we've come?" she murmured; her voice filled with wonder. "This place feels so different now, so full of hope and possibility."

Daniel kissed the top of her head, his heart swelling with pride and affection. "It's incredible," he agreed. "And it's all because of you, Emily. Your strength, your compassion—they've been the driving force behind this transformation."

Emily looked up at him, her eyes shining with love. "We did this together, Daniel. I couldn't have done it without you. Your unwavering support and love have meant everything to me."

Daniel smiled, his eyes reflecting the depth of his feelings. "I love you, Emily. More than words can express. And I can't wait to see what the future holds for us."

As they stood together, lost in their thoughts, the door to the grand hall creaked open, and Jack and Grace walked in, their faces radiant with happiness. They had been inseparable since the night of the final ritual, their love blossoming amidst the newfound peace of the mansion.

"Good morning, lovebirds," Jack teased, his eyes twinkling with amusement. "Hope we're not interrupting."

Emily laughed, the sound filled with joy. "Not at all, Jack. We were just reflecting on everything that's happened."

Grace nodded, her expression thoughtful. "It's amazing, isn't it? How much has changed in such a short time. This place feels like a completely different world."

Jack wrapped an arm around her shoulders, pulling her close. "And it's all thanks to the incredible teamwork and love we've shared. We've built something truly special here."

Emily smiled, feeling a deep sense of gratitude for the friendships that had formed during their journey. "We've all grown so much, and we've learned that love and unity can overcome even the darkest of times."

The four of them stood together, basking in the warm glow of their shared success. The mansion, once a symbol of sorrow and loss, was now a testament to the power of love, resilience, and community.

As the days turned into weeks, the transformation of the mansion continued. The community members, inspired by the journey they had all undertaken, worked together to restore the mansion to its former glory. Each room was filled with light and laughter, the walls echoing with the sounds of friendship and joy.

Emily and Daniel found themselves at the center of this new beginning, their love serving as a guiding light for those around them. They hosted gatherings and events, bringing people together and fostering a sense of unity and belonging.

One evening, as the sun set and the sky was painted with hues of pink and orange, Emily and Daniel found themselves alone in the garden. The flowers, carefully tended by Grace and Jack, were in full bloom, their vibrant colors a symbol of the renewal and hope that had taken root in the mansion.

Daniel took Emily's hand, his touch gentle and reassuring. "I have a surprise for you," he said, his voice filled with excitement.

Emily's eyes sparkled with curiosity. "Oh? What is it?"

Daniel led her to a secluded corner of the garden, where a small table was set up, adorned with candles and a bouquet of roses. A bottle of champagne sat chilling in a silver bucket, and two glasses were placed neatly on the table.

"Daniel, this is beautiful," Emily whispered, her heart swelling with love.

Daniel smiled, his eyes never leaving hers. "I wanted to celebrate everything we've accomplished, and to toast to our future together."

As they sat down and poured the champagne, Daniel raised his glass, his voice filled with emotion. "To us, Emily. To our love, our strength, and the beautiful journey we've shared. I can't wait to see what the future holds for us."

Emily clinked her glass against his, her eyes shining with tears of happiness. "To us, Daniel. And to the incredible life we're building together."

They sipped their champagne, the bubbles tickling their tongues, and reveled in the beauty of the moment. The garden, bathed in the soft glow of the candles, felt like a magical oasis, a testament to the power of love and resilience.

As the night wore on, they talked about their dreams and aspirations, the plans they had for the mansion and their future. They spoke of the community they had built, the friendships that had blossomed, and the love that had carried them through the darkest of times.

Emily leaned against Daniel, feeling a profound sense of peace and contentment. "We've come so far, Daniel. And I know that whatever challenges we face in the future, we'll face them together."

Daniel kissed her forehead, his heart filled with love. "Always, Emily. We'll face everything together, with love and determination."

Daniel wrapped his arms around Emily and kissed her deeply. "I am so lucky to have you," he said, his hands wandering down to Emily's ass.

Emily giggled and pulled away. "Come on, let's go inside," she said, taking Daniel's hand.

Daniel continued there, began undressing Emily. Daniel watched as Emily's eyes sparkled with excitement, and he felt his cock growing hard in his pants.

Emily pulled Daniel's shirt over his head and began kissing his chest. Daniel groaned as Emily's lips moved lower, her tongue tracing a path down his stomach.

Emily looked up at Daniel, her eyes filled with desire. "I want you to make love to me," she whispered.

Daniel didn't need to be asked twice. He quickly stripped off the rest of his clothes and climbed onto the small bed, positioning himself above Emily.

Emily looked up at Daniel, her eyes filled with anticipation. Daniel leaned down and kissed her deeply, his hands exploring her body.

Emily wrapped her legs around Daniel's waist, pulling him closer. Daniel could feel Emily's warmth against his cock, and he knew he couldn't wait any longer.

Daniel entered Emily slowly, savoring the feeling of her tight pussy around him. Emily moaned as Daniel filled her, her nails digging into his back.

Daniel began to move, his hips rocking back and forth as he made love to Emily. Emily looked up at Daniel, her eyes filled with pleasure as he fucked her.

Daniel leaned down and kissed Emily, his tongue exploring her mouth as he continued to fuck her. Emily moaned, her hips meeting Daniel's as they moved together in a rhythm that was both primal and beautiful.

Daniel could feel himself getting close to the edge, and he knew he needed to make this moment last. He slowed down, his hips moving in slow, deliberate strokes as he made love to Emily.

Emily looked up at Daniel, her eyes filled with desire. "I want you to come inside me," she whispered.

Daniel groaned, his hips quickening as he felt himself getting closer to the edge. Emily moaned, her pussy tightening around Daniel's cock as he fucked her harder.

Daniel could feel himself about to cum, and he knew he needed to make this moment last. He slowed down, his hips moving in slow, deliberate strokes as he made love to Emily.

Emily looked up at Daniel, her eyes filled with desire. "I want you to come inside me," she whispered.

Daniel groaned, his hips quickening as he felt himself getting closer to the edge. Emily moaned, her pussy tightening around Daniel's cock as he fucked her harder.

Daniel could feel himself about to cum, and he knew he needed to make this moment last. He slowed down, his hips moving in slow, deliberate strokes as he made love to Emily.

Daniel groaned, his hips quickening as he felt himself getting closer to the edge. He fucked her harder and cum inside Emily. Still thinking about Grace.

As they sat together under the stars, surrounded by the beauty of the garden and the warmth of their love, Emily knew that their journey was far from over. But she also knew that with Daniel by her side, there was nothing they couldn't overcome.

The mansion, once a place of darkness and sorrow, was now a beacon of hope and love. And as Emily looked around at the faces of their friends and neighbors, she knew that their story was only just beginning.

Together, they had created a place of light and love, a testament to the power of unity and resilience. And as they embarked on this new chapter of their lives, Emily and Daniel knew that their love would continue to guide them, lighting the way to a future filled with hope and happiness.

Chapter 15: A New Dawn

The first light of dawn gently bathed the mansion in a soft, golden hue, casting long shadows that stretched across the dewy grass of the garden. Emily and Daniel stood on the porch, their hands intertwined, watching as the sun slowly rose above the horizon, signaling the start of a new day and a new chapter in their lives.

Emily turned to Daniel, her eyes reflecting the warm glow of the sunrise. "Can you believe how far we've come?" she whispered, her voice filled with awe and gratitude. "From darkness and despair to this—our beautiful home, filled with love and hope."

Daniel smiled, his gaze never leaving hers. "It's hard to believe sometimes, but when I look at you, I know everything we've been through has led us to this moment. Our love has transformed this place, and it will continue to guide us through whatever comes next."

As the sun climbed higher, its rays illuminating the mansion and its surroundings, Jack and Grace emerged from the garden, their faces beaming with joy. They had spent the early morning hours tending to the flowers, ensuring that every bloom reflected the vibrancy and life that had returned to the mansion.

"Good morning, you two," Jack called out, his voice filled with cheer. "Ready for another beautiful day?"

Emily laughed, her heart light with happiness. "Good morning, Jack, Grace. It's a perfect day, isn't it?"

Grace nodded, her eyes sparkling. "It is. And it's just the beginning. There's so much more to look forward to."

They all stood together on the porch, the rising sun casting a warm glow over them, symbolizing the promise of new beginnings and endless possibilities. The mansion, once a place of darkness and sorrow, was now a beacon of hope, love, and unity.

A few days later, Emily prepared for another visit to her Aunt Margaret, who had been a source of comfort and wisdom during their journey. The time spent with her aunt had been healing for both of them, and Emily was eager to share the latest news and to ensure her aunt was well.

Daniel helped her pack, his hands gentle as he placed her belongings into the suitcase. "I'll miss you," he said softly, his eyes filled with love and a hint of sadness. "But I know how important this is for you and your aunt."

Emily smiled, cupping his cheek with her hand. "I'll miss you too, Daniel. But I'll be back before you know it. And I know Grace will take good care of you while I'm gone."

Grace, who was assisting with the preparations, nodded reassuringly. "Don't worry, Emily. I've got everything under control. Daniel will be well looked after."

They all shared a heartfelt embrace, the bond between them stronger than ever. As Emily set off on her journey, Daniel stood on the porch, waving until she disappeared from sight, his heart aching with the temporary separation but filled with confidence in their love.

With Emily away, Grace took her role as caretaker seriously, ensuring Daniel was comfortable and well-fed. They spent their days working in the garden, tending to the flowers and enjoying the tranquility that now permeated the mansion.

One afternoon, as they were pruning roses, Daniel slipped on the damp grass and twisted his ankle. Grace was at his side in an instant, her hands gentle as she helped him to a nearby bench.

"Are you alright?" she asked, concern etched on her face.

Daniel winced, but managed a smile. "I'll be fine, Grace. Just a little tumble."

Grace fetched a cold compress and some ointment from the house, applying it to his ankle with care. "You need to rest for a bit. No more gardening for today."

Daniel chuckled, appreciating her care. "Yes, ma'am. I'll take it easy. Hey Grace, about the other day. It was a moment of passion, some sudden burst of energy that I had seeing you chanting. I hope you liked it."

"Yes, I loved it, Daniel?" she said. "I know you are deeply in love with mam, and I respect it and will not tell about it to anyone. No one has treated me with respect like you, Daniel. So, I am all yours."

Meanwhile, Jack had to make a trip to the city to gather supplies for the library, which they were restoring to its former glory. He promised to return in two days, leaving with a list of books and artifacts that would enrich the mansion's collection.

It was the third day of Emily's vacation, and Daniel was lounging in the hot tub, his body glistening with water. Grace walked out to the backyard, wearing a skimpy skirt that left little to the imagination. Daniel's eyes trailed down her body, taking in every curve and angle.

Grace walked over to the hot tub, her hips swaying seductively. Removing her skirt, she climbed in, sitting across from Daniel. She leaned back, her breasts barely contained by the tiny triangles of fabric. Daniel couldn't help but stare, his cock already starting to harden.

"I think it's time for another round," she whispered.

Daniel nodded, his heart racing. Grace straddled him, her legs on either side of his waist. She ground her hips against him, and he groaned, his hands automatically going to her ass.

They kissed, their tongues exploring each other's mouths. Grace reached down, pulling Daniel's swim trunks down just enough to free his cock. She stroked him, her grip tight and firm. Daniel moaned, his head falling back against the edge of the hot tub.

Grace moved her hips, positioning herself above Daniel's cock. She slowly lowered herself down, taking him inside her. Daniel gasped, his fingers digging into her ass.

They started to move, their bodies rocking together in a steady rhythm. The water sloshed around them, splashing over the sides of the hot tub. Daniel's hands roamed over Grace's body, cupping her breasts, tracing the curve of her hips.

Grace leaned back, her head thrown back in pleasure. Daniel watched her, his eyes taking in every inch of her exposed skin. He reached up, pinching her nipples between his fingers. She moaned, her pussy clenching around his cock.

Daniel couldn't hold back any longer. He thrust up into her, his orgasm building in his balls. Grace cried out, her pussy tightening around him. Daniel groaned, emptying himself inside her.

They sat there for a moment; their bodies still connected. Grace leaned forward, kissing Daniel softly.

Grace noticed, and she reached out, running her hand along Daniel's thigh. He shivered, goosebumps breaking out on his skin. She moved closer, her lips brushing against his ear.

In the evening, Grace was preparing food. Daniel made his way to the kitchen, his footsteps quietly on the tile floor. Daniel pushed Grace up against the counter, his body pressed against h. She reached down, pulling his trunks the rest of the way off. Daniel kicked them aside, his hands automatically going to Grace's skirt.

They stripped each other quickly, their need for each other overpowering. Grace climbed onto the counter; her legs spread wide. Daniel stepped between them, his cock already hard again.

He entered her slowly, savoring the feeling of her tight pussy around him. Grace moaned; her head thrown back. Daniel started to move, his hips thrusting in a steady rhythm.

Grace reached down, her fingers finding her clit. She rubbed it in slow circles, her orgasm building. Daniel watched her, his own pleasure building.

Grace came first, her pussy clenching around Daniel's cock. He groaned, his own orgasm following close behind. They collapsed onto the counter; their bodies spent. "Can you stay here tonight" asked Daniel.

"I can come back early morning, if you want. Night, I have to take care of dad at home." said Grace.

"Ok, that is fine, morning is good", said Daniel.

Next morning, Daniel woke up early to find Grace in his bedroom. She was getting into his bed, and Daniel was waiting for this moment. He watched as she took off her maid uniform, revealing her naked body. Daniel felt his dick getting hard as he stared at her perfect ass.

Grace turned to Daniel and smiled. "Good morning, Daniel," she said. "I thought we could have a little fun this morning."

She came to bed and started grinding her hips against his dick, and Daniel reached up and grabbed her breasts, squeezing them gently as she continued to ride him.

Grace leaned down and whispered in Daniel's ear. "Do you want to fuck my ass, Daniel?" she asked.

Daniel nodded his head eagerly. He had always wanted to try anal sex, but he had never had the chance. He watched as Grace got off of him and turned around, positioning herself so that her ass was facing him.

Daniel positioned himself behind her and slowly pushed himself inside of her. It felt amazing, and Daniel couldn't believe how tight Grace's ass was. He started thrusting harder and harder, and Grace moaned with pleasure.

"Fuck, Daniel, you feel so good inside of me," she said.

Daniel couldn't believe how good it felt to be inside of Grace's ass. He had never felt anything like it before. He continued to thrust harder and harder, and soon he could feel himself getting close to Cumming.

"I'm going to cum, Grace," he said.

Grace turned to him and smiled. "Cum inside of me, Daniel," she said.

Daniel nodded his head and continued to thrust. He could feel himself getting closer and closer to cumming, and soon he was there. He let out a loud moan as he filled Grace's ass with his cum.

Grace turned to him and smiled. "That was amazing, Daniel," she said.

Daniel couldn't agree more. He had never had a better sexual experience in his life. He couldn't wait to do it again.

"Thank you, Grace," he said. "That was incredible."

Grace smiled and leaned in to kiss him. "Anytime, Daniel," she said.

Daniel and Grace continued to have sex for the rest of the morning. It was the best morning of Daniel's life, and he knew that he would never forget it. He was grateful to have a maid like Grace who was always willing to satisfy his sexual desires.

The next few days passed quickly. Grace took excellent care of Daniel, ensuring he rested his ankle and kept his spirits high. They spent their evenings on the porch, talking and sharing stories, the bond between them growing stronger.

One morning, Daniel suggested they tackle the cleanup of the basement and the hidden tunnels—a task they had put off for far too long. Grace agreed, eager to uncover any remaining secrets of the mansion.

The basement was dimly lit and filled with old, dusty furniture, crates, and cobwebs. Grace and Daniel worked side by side, sorting through the forgotten relics of the past. They discovered old letters, photographs, and even some ancient artifacts that added to the rich history of the mansion.

As they moved deeper into the basement, they found a hidden door leading to the tunnels beneath the mansion. Armed with flashlights and a sense of adventure, they ventured into the dark, narrow passageways. The air was cool and musty, and their footsteps echoed off the stone walls.

"This place is incredible," Grace whispered, her voice filled with awe. "It's like stepping back in time."

Daniel nodded, shining his flashlight on the walls, which were covered in faded markings and symbols. "There's so much history here. I'm glad we're doing this together."

As they explored the tunnels, they uncovered hidden chambers and passageways that led to different parts of the mansion. Each discovery added another layer to the story of the mansion, deepening their connection to its past.

In one chamber, they found an old chest filled with journals and letters that told the stories of the mansion's previous inhabitants. Grace and Daniel read through the pages, piecing together the lives and loves of those who had come before them.

"This is amazing," Grace said, her eyes shining with excitement. "These people lived, loved, and faced their own challenges just like us."

Daniel smiled, feeling a deep sense of gratitude for the journey they were on. "And now their stories are a part of ours. We're continuing their legacy."

After hours of exploration and discovery, they emerged from the tunnels, covered in dust but filled with a sense of accomplishment. They had not only uncovered the hidden secrets of the mansion but had also strengthened their bond through their shared adventure.

As the sun set, casting a golden glow over the mansion, Grace and Daniel sat on the porch, reflecting on their day's work. The garden was bathed in the soft light of dusk, and the air was filled with the scent of blooming flowers.

"Thank you for today, Grace," Daniel said, his voice filled with sincerity. "I couldn't have done it without you."

Grace smiled, her heart full. "It was my pleasure, Daniel. We're all in this together, and I'm grateful to be a part of it."

They sat in companionable silence, watching the stars appear in the night sky. The mansion, once a place of darkness and sorrow, was now a symbol of hope, love, and new beginnings. And as they looked out over the transformed home, they knew that their journey was far from over.

Grace got up and hugged Daniel from behind. Daniel felt Grace's nipples harden under her dress as she pressed her chest against his back. Her hand snaked down his chest and under the waistband of his boxers, fingers searching for his cock. He smiled as he felt her fingers wrap around his throbbing erection, his ass grinding back against her as she started to stroke him.

Grace had been Daniel's maid for over a year now, but she had never been this forward before. Her hand on his cock felt amazing, and he could feel his balls start to tighten as she quickened her pace. He reached back and grabbed her ass, pulling her closer to him, feeling her breasts press against his back as he started to grind his hips back against her.

She reached down and grabbed the waistband of his boxers, pulling them down over his hips and letting them fall to the floor. His cock sprang free, throbbing and erect, and she reached down and wrapped her hand around it, stroking him slowly as they kissed.

Daniel reached down and grabbed her by the thighs, lifting her up and wrapping her legs around his waist. She moaned as he carried her over to the bed, laying her down on her back and climbing on top of her.

He kissed his way down her body, his lips brushing against her neck and collarbone before moving down to her breasts. He took one of her nipples in his mouth, sucking on it gently as she arched her back and moaned. He reached down and slipped a finger inside her pussy, feeling her wetness coat his finger as he started to stroke her.

She reached down and grabbed his cock, guiding it to her entrance. He pushed inside her slowly, feeling her tightness wrap around his cock as he started to thrust in and out of her. She moaned, her fingers digging into his shoulders as he picked up the pace, his hips slapping against hers as he fucked her.

Just as he felt his climax building, he heard the door to his room open. He looked up to see Emily standing in the doorway, her eyes wide as she took in the sight of him fucking Grace.

"Oh, fuck," he groaned, his hips stuttering as he tried to pull out of Grace. But she grabbed onto his hips, holding him in place as she started to grind her hips against his.

"What's going on here?" Emily's voice was sharp, filled with confusion and hurt.

Daniel looked up, surprised and concern in his eyes. "Emily, you're back! I hurt my ankle while you were away, and Grace has been helping me. Trust me this was the only once we had it."

Emily's eyes flicked between the two of them. "It looks like you've gotten very close," she said, her voice trembling. "Why didn't you tell me about this?"

"I need some air," Emily said, her voice barely above a whisper. She turned and hurried out of the room, the walls of the mansion feeling suddenly constricting.

Daniel struggled to get off the bed, wincing in pain. "Emily, wait!" he called out, but she was already halfway down the stairs.

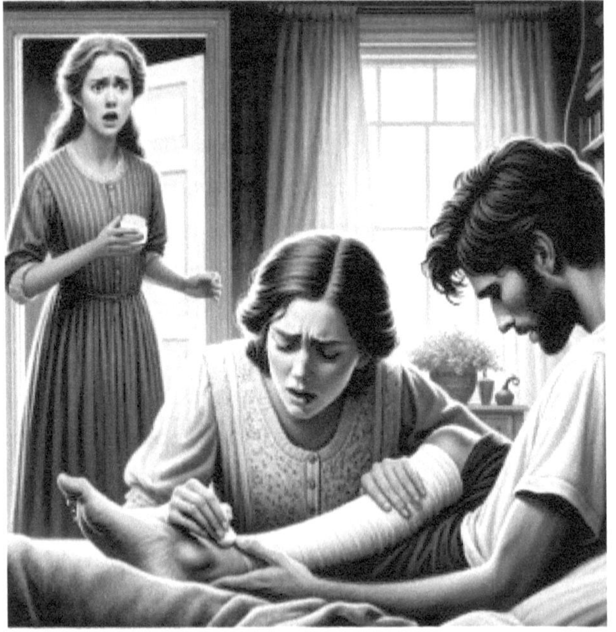

Emily found herself in the garden, the fresh air doing little to calm her racing heart. She sat on a bench, tears streaming down her face. She felt a hand on her shoulder and looked up to see Daniel standing there, concern etched on his face.

Daniel took a deep breath. "I hurt my ankle while you were gone, and Grace has been taking care of me. This was a moment of passion and there's nothing more to it. I promise you, Emily, my heart belongs to you and only you."

"I believe you," she said finally, her voice soft. "It's just... seeing you two together like that, it was a shock. I will show you how it feels when your love is not honest with you. Tell me how you will feel if I fuck Jack in front of you to make it even."

Daniel was silent and was guilty of what he did.

Chapter 15: A Fractured Trust

As the first light of dawn bathed the mansion in a soft, golden hue, Emily stood on the porch, her heart heavy with the events of the previous day. The image of Grace and Daniel together on the bed still burned in her mind, despite their explanations and reassurances. The trust she had so carefully nurtured felt fragile and frayed.

Determined to take control of her emotions, Emily decided on a course of action that would make Daniel understand the depth of her hurt. She found Grace in the kitchen, preparing breakfast.

"Grace," Emily said, her voice cold and resolute. Grace looked up, her eyes wide with surprise and concern. "I need to talk to you."

Grace set down the knife she was holding and wiped her hands on a towel. "Of course, Emily. What is it?"

Emily stepped closer, her eyes blazing with a mix of anger and resolve. "I want you to know how it feels to have your trust betrayed. I'm going to make love to Jack tonight. I want you to feel the same pain I felt."

Grace's face paled, her eyes filling with tears. "Emily, please, you don't have to do this. Nothing happened between Daniel and me. It was all innocent, just one time."

Emily's heart ached, but she held firm. "I need to do this, Grace. I need to show you how it feels."

Leaving Grace in the kitchen, Emily made her way to the library, where she knew Jack would be working. She found him hunched over a stack of books, his expression focused and intense.

"Jack," she said softly, stepping into the room. Jack looked up, a warm smile spreading across his face.

"Emily, welcome back," he greeted, setting aside his work. "How was your visit with your aunt?"

"It was good," Emily replied, her voice steady. "But I've found some more secrets in one of the hidden rooms in the basement. Can you come back tonight? I want to show you what I've discovered."

Jack's curiosity was piqued, and he nodded eagerly. "Of course, Emily. I'll be here."

As the evening approached, Emily's resolve hardened. She knew her plan was risky and could cause more harm than good, but the desire to make Daniel and Grace understand her pain was overwhelming.

Jack arrived as promised, and Emily led him to the basement, careful to avoid arousing Daniel's suspicion. Daniel was working in his home office, absorbed in his tasks, while Grace busied herself in the kitchen, her mind undoubtedly preoccupied with Emily's earlier words.

As they descended into the dimly lit basement, Emily's heart pounded with a mixture of guilt and determination. She knew Jack trusted her implicitly, and the thought of using that trust to make her point gnawed at her conscience.

"Here it is," Emily said, guiding Jack to the hidden room she had mentioned. "I found these old journals and artifacts that I think you'll find fascinating."

Jack's eyes lit up with excitement as he examined the items. "This is incredible, Emily. Thank you for sharing this with me."

As Jack immersed himself in the discoveries, Emily took a deep breath, steeling herself for what she was about to do. She stepped closer to Jack, her fingers brushing against his arm.

"Jack," she said softly, her voice trembling. "There's something else I need to share with you."

Jack looked up, his expression curious and concerned. "What is it, Emily?"

Emily's eyes filled with tears as she reached out to touch his cheek. "I need to show you something... something that will make you understand."

Before Jack could respond, Emily pressed her lips to his, her kiss filled with a mix of desperation and determination. Jack stiffened in surprise, his eyes wide with shock.

"Emily, what are you doing?" he gasped, pulling away slightly.

Emily's tears fell freely now, her voice breaking. "I'm sorry, Jack. I need to show Daniel and Grace how it feels to have their trust betrayed."

Jack's expression softened with understanding and compassion. "Emily, this isn't the way. You don't need to hurt yourself or others to prove a point."

But Emily's mind was made up, and she kissed him again, more fervently this time. Jack, despite his reservations, couldn't deny the connection he felt with her. He returned the kiss, their emotions tangled in a whirlwind of confusion and passion.

Upstairs, the sounds from the basement reached Daniel's ears. He paused, his heart sinking as he realized what was happening. He rushed to the kitchen, finding Grace there, her face pale and eyes filled with tears.

"Daniel," she whispered, her voice choked with emotion. "Emily told me she was going to do this. She wanted to punish us."

Daniel's heart ached with the weight of Emily's pain. He hurried to the basement; Grace close behind him. As they reached the bottom of the stairs, the sight of naked Emily and forcing Jack stopped them in their tracks.

"Emily, stop!" Daniel called out; his voice filled with desperation.

Emily pulled away from Jack, her eyes wide with shock and sorrow. "Daniel, I..."

Daniel crossed the room, his eyes searching hers. "I understand, Emily. I understand your pain. But this isn't the way."

Grace stepped forward, her voice gentle but firm. "Emily, we love you. And we need to work through this together."

Emily's resolve crumbled, and she collapsed into Daniel's arms, her tears flowing freely. "I'm so sorry," she sobbed. "I just wanted you to feel what I felt."

Daniel held her tightly, his own tears mingling with hers. "I know, Emily. And I'm sorry for the hurt I've caused. But we can get through this. Together."

Jack stood by, his heart heavy with the weight of the situation. Grace moved to his side, offering silent support.

As the four of them stood together in the dimly lit basement, the walls of the mansion seemed to close in, but the strength of their love and commitment to each other created a space of healing and understanding.

They knew the road ahead would be difficult, but they also knew that they had the power to rebuild their trust and move forward, united by their shared journey and the love that bound them.

Chapter 16: Happily, Ever After

The sun rose gently over the mansion, casting a golden glow over its restored façade. Inside, the air was thick with tension and unspoken words. Emily had spent a restless night, her mind racing with the events of the past few days. The sight of Grace and Daniel together had left her feeling hurt and betrayed, even though their intentions had been innocent, and it was one time passion.

That morning, in the grand hall where so many significant moments had taken place, Emily stood waiting. Her heart was heavy, but she was determined to confront her feelings and find a resolution.

She didn't have to wait long before Daniel, Grace, and Jack joined her, each carrying their own burdens of guilt and worry.

Daniel was the first to speak, his voice filled with remorse. "Emily, I am so sorry for everything. I never meant to hurt you. Grace was just helping me with my injury, and I should have been more open with you about it. I love you more than anything, and I promise this will never happen again."

Grace stepped forward; her eyes filled with tears. "Emily, I would never betray your trust. Daniel means a lot to me, but only as a friend and master. I'm truly sorry for the pain I've caused you."

Emily felt her emotions swell up, and she couldn't hold back her tears any longer. They flowed freely, her shoulders shaking with the intensity of her feelings. "I was so scared," she sobbed. "I felt like everything we built was falling apart. But I believe you both. I just... I need to heal from this."

Daniel moved closer, wrapping his arms around her. "We'll get through this together, Emily. I promise you that."

Grace added softly, "I'll do whatever it takes to regain your trust, Emily."

Jack, who had been quietly supportive throughout the ordeal, stepped forward and placed a gentle hand on Emily's shoulder. "It's okay to be hurt, Emily. But we're all here for you, and we'll help you heal."

Emily looked up at Jack, gratitude mingling with her tears. "I'm sorry, Jack. I dragged you into this mess."

Jack shook his head. "You have nothing to apologize for, Emily. We're all in this together."

Over the next few days, the mansion slowly returned to its usual rhythm. The air was filled with the sounds of laughter and conversation as Emily, Daniel, Grace, and Jack worked together to restore the mansion and its grounds. The hurt and betrayal that had hung over them began to dissipate, replaced by a renewed sense of unity and understanding.

Emily found herself growing closer to Grace, their shared experiences forging a bond that transcended the pain of the past. They spent hours talking and laughing, their friendship stronger than ever.

One afternoon, as they tended to the garden, Emily turned to Grace and said, "Thank you for being here for me. I know it wasn't easy, but I'm glad we worked through it. Was it really one time. I will trust you whatever the answer is."

Grace smiled warmly. "I'm grateful too, Emily. Our friendship means a lot to me. Yes, it was just one time, and I was drawn into the moment. Daniel did not start, I did, and I am sorry for that. Daniel really loves you.", Grace lied.

Emily felt relieved. A burden off her chest and she hugged Grace. For the first time she noticed that Grace not only is a beautiful lady but also has a very voluptuous body. She kept her in embrace for few minutes and she enjoyed the feeling of tight embrace with a woman. After some time, she let her go. Grace felt a little odd with the embrace but enjoyed it as well. Before going she hugged her again, this time only for a short time.

Meanwhile, Daniel and Jack focused on the mansion's library, cataloging the new books and artifacts Jack had brought back from the city. Their camaraderie was palpable, their shared efforts bringing a sense of accomplishment and joy.

As the sun set one evening, casting a warm glow over the garden, Emily and Daniel stood together, hand in hand. They watched as Jack and Grace laughed and worked side by side, their own bond growing stronger with each passing day.

"We've come a long way," Daniel said softly, his voice filled with pride and love.

Emily nodded; her heart full. "We have. And I'm so grateful for everything we have. For you, for our friends, and for this beautiful home we've created."

Daniel turned to her, his eyes shining with love. "I promise you, Emily, I'll never take our love for granted again. You've given me everything, and I intend to cherish it forever."

Emily leaned in, their lips meeting in a tender kiss that spoke of forgiveness, love, and a future filled with promise.

That night, as they gathered in the grand hall for a simple dinner, surrounded by friends and filled with laughter, Emily felt a deep sense of peace. The mansion, once a place of shadows and secrets, was now a beacon of love and hope. Emily and Daniel went to bed together and slept in a tight embrace for the whole night.

The bonds they had forged were unbreakable, their love stronger than ever. Together, they faced the future with open hearts and unwavering faith in each other.

As the candles flickered and the stars twinkled above, Emily knew that their journey was far from over. But whatever challenges lay ahead, they would face them together, united by love and strengthened by their shared experiences.

And so, as the night enveloped the mansion in its gentle embrace, Emily, Daniel, Grace, and Jack looked forward to a future filled with light, love, and endless possibilities.

Their happily ever after was just the beginning of a new adventure.

| Page

About the Author

Candy Christie is an emerging author making her mark in the world of romance novels. With a few heartfelt books to her name, she has quickly captured the attention of readers who appreciate stories filled with emotional depth, vivid characters, and the timeless theme of love conquering all.

Growing up in a picturesque coastal town, Candy was inspired by the beauty around her and the rich tapestry of human experiences. This inspiration is evident in her writing, where she skillfully brings to life the settings and characters that resonate with authenticity and warmth. Her love for classic literature and a lifelong passion for storytelling led her to pursue a career in writing, where she finds joy in creating compelling narratives that touch the hearts of her readers.

Before embarking on her journey as a novelist, Candy worked in journalism, where she honed her skills in storytelling and character development. This background provided her with a strong foundation for her transition to writing fiction, allowing her to craft intricate plots and deeply relatable characters.

Candy's debut novel was met with enthusiasm from readers and critics alike, establishing her as a promising new voice in the romance genre. Her subsequent books have continued to build her reputation, each one showcasing her ability to weave together romance, suspense, and richly developed characters.

When she's not writing, Candy enjoys exploring the natural beauty of her hometown, painting, and spending time with her family and friends. She is also passionate about supporting literacy programs and inspiring a love of reading and writing in others.

Candy Christie's novels are a testament to the power of love, healing, and new beginnings. With each book, she invites readers to join her on a journey of passion and discovery, leaving them eagerly anticipating her next enchanting story.